THE GOSSAMER FLY

Meira Chand was born and educated in London. Her mother is Swiss, and her father is Indian. She trained as a textile designer. She is married to an Indian businessman and they have lived in Japan since 1962, except for a brief period in India. *The Gossamer Fly* is her first novel.

ARENA

Also in Arena by Meira Chand
THE BONSAI TREE

Meira Chand

THE GOSSAMER FLY

An Arena Book
Published by Arrow Books Limited
62-65 Chandos Place, London WC2N 4NW

An imprint of Century Hutchinson Ltd

London Melbourne Sydney Auckland
Johannesburg and agencies throughout
the world

First published in Great Britain by
John Murray (Publishers) Limited 1979
Century paperback edition 1984
Arena edition 1986

Printed and bound in Great Britain by
The Guernsey Press Ltd, Guernsey, C.I.

ISBN 0 09 950720 X

.... that intangible thing they call a gossamer-fly flitted across his path.

'Now you are caught' I cried, and
        thought I held it safe.
But when I looked the gossamer-fly
        had vanished –
vanished or never been in my hand.'

Such was the poem that he recited, sitting alone.

The Tale of Genji by **Lady Murasaki**

For
Nissim Ezekiel

[1]

That Summer was a first growing up. And after it the rustle of grass, the view of the bay, each thing she touched were never the same, but filled with the menace of a dark adult world. Like a ceiling upon a tall room.

Then, it was the tick of the clock, unswerving, going on after everything stopped, which possessed her nightmares. That, and the russet iron faces of Japanese armour standing in her father's study. These walked forever towards her, slowly. Each step a clump of metallic scales and a ripple of shoulder flaps, as if a wind were caught beneath. Their faces, carved in flanges and ridges, were ferocious as the wind god. The blue laced one had a sparse white beard, the other a hog-hair moustache. But their eyes were the same, empty dead slits, blacker than their faces.

In her mind everything began on that first day, when she found the new maid, Hiroko, in the kitchen, with chopsticks pulling white flakes of fish from the bones, eating her lunch. The room smelled of yellow radish pickle and the fish, charred on a wire stand over a flame. Hiroko picked up a slice of pickle between wooden chopsticks, and took a sharp bite. She did this exactly, taking her time, ignoring Natsuko who had come into the room and stood near the table. Finally she raised her head.

'Are you the daughter? You look like your mother.' Her eyes were still, without expression, staring across the table.

'Is your mother American or English? It's strange you're

9

blonde like her, and don't have your father's Japanese hair. My sister once worked in an orphanage for half-blood Japanese children, after the war. I went there once. I must have been your age, nine or ten. I saw all kind of weird faces, especially the ones with Negro fathers. But I never saw any with hair like yours.' Hiroko looked at Natsuko critically, and gave a sudden harsh laugh.

Immediately then Natsuko knew she would not like her. And that, for some reason of her own, Hiroko had decided this. Still, she sat the other side of the table and watched across a green checked cloth. But Hiroko continued to observe her silently, until Natsuko felt yellow and thin, rinsed through by inexplicable shame. Then, still without speaking, Hiroko took another bite of pickle, and returned her gaze to the food. Natsuko watched the lower half of her face, moving elastically to the crunch of radish.

Three days before her parents had interviewed Hiroko. Afterwards Natsuko slipped quietly into the lounge. She sat on the floor, running a finger around a stain on the surface of an occasional table. Shutting the front door behind Hiroko, Natsuko's mother came slowly back into the room.

'No,' she said, shaking her head. 'I do not like her. She is not the right type. Unless we are careful she will have men, all kinds, through the back window.'

She said the words primly, but her eyes fixed boldly upon her husband. In the chair she leaned wearily, blonde hair hanging limply to the curve of her jaw.

'She has worked in a tearoom, a bar, a factory and one of those dreadful neon-lighted cabarets in Shinshaibashi. She could have been a stripper for all we know. What does she want to come here for? It strikes me always, there are only two types of women here in Japan. The wives and the bar girls. Ladies or sluts. It is quite clear in which category Hiroko fits.'

Kazuo Akazawa closed his book with an abrupt snap. 'You are bigoted Frances, and quite wrong in your attitude to Japanese women. But what shall we do? You know how hard it is to find help. You seem unable to manage the house any longer yourself. You've been tired and unwell for a long time now. Nobody else answered our advertisement. If you would only not be so obstinately proud and ask my family, they might find somebody with a recommendation. That would be best.' His expression prepared for a new chapter of friction.

At once Frances Akazawa's eyes flicked open. 'No. I will not ask. We will keep her. We will try. She may be all right, you never know.'

She said it quickly, twisting her rings. Knotting restless hands in her lap, she closed her eyes upon it all. Kazuo shrugged, pursed his lips and reopened his book. Silence filled the room. They sat in their chairs, cold and hard, while unsaid words bobbed and sank between them.

Crouched at the table Natsuko examined inlaid chips of mother of pearl, smelling the unhealthy odour. Later the words would break out, cracking and frothing, like frozen water in a bottle. In bed in the dark, she would lie and hear it all. It was the same each night. Even with her head beneath the pillow the angry splinters and lacerated words sank into her, filling her body with fear and pain. The decision was no victory for her mother, just another tired weight, and a colder tightening to her father's mouth.

Hiroko's half-eaten sphere of pickle rested on top of a mound of rice. From its centre a grainy texture radiated out, faintly, like a watermark. Lipstick smudged the bitten edge. Opening off the kitchen was the small room Natsuko had helped her mother clear for Hiroko the day before. Besides the vacuum cleaner and ironing board, a disused birdcage, cushions, carrier bags and boxes of oddments were pulled from the room. Also a large metal trunk that had accompanied the Akazawas on the boat to Japan, after they met and married in England. Frances greeted each object with a groan, wondering where to dispose of it. At last the room was clear and curtains hung at the window. Natsuko found a wall vase, decorated with a garish picture of *geisha*, and filled it with two pink camellia from the garden.

The door was open, the room unoccupied yet by Hiroko. Her belongings stood in the middle of the floor; a cardboard box done up with blue string and two large bundles tied in brightly patterned carrying cloths. Dumping them there she had come immediately into the kitchen to eat. Sodden newspaper wrapping from the fish lay on the draining board, the white a dull wet grey. Up on the table, in the metal lunch box, were the rice and pickles she had brought with her. And Natsuko noticed their own blue flowered teapot, the smallest one, a faint line of steam drifting from the spout. There was no sound now from the radish in Hiroko's mouth, just a few softened yellow particles stuck around her teeth.

But staring at the table Natsuko thought, she has opened the cupboards, found the pot and the box of green tea leaves. All this she has done by herself, without help. Pushing into their cupboards, touching cups, moving plates and glasses, looking behind neat piles for the teapot. Her presence disturbed the kitchen, something new pervaded the air. Its ownership was shared.

Lifting the pot by its wicker handle, Hiroko poured tea into a small bowl. A leaf swirled up to the surface and disappeared instantly beneath the stream. Taking the bowl in both hands she sipped loudly several times, and then looked directly at Natsuko.

'Now you had better show me around,' she said, standing up.

Together they walked through the house, Natsuko in front. From behind came the flip flop of Hiroko's felt slippers. In woollen socks Natsuko's own feet slipped upon the polished wood. Thin gaps between the boards pressed into the flesh of her heel, cold and hard. Trailing behind, Hiroko commented at the number and size of rooms, the length of passages, at the dirt on top of picture frames. But in the study, before the two suits of armour, sitting side by side in front of a screen, the sword collection upon the wall, and the glassed shelves of books, she stood a moment, silent. Then, from the back of her throat came a short harsh note of surprise, like a bird. Natsuko was pleased, in spite of her own dislike of the house. For the sunless rooms and passages, the shiny panelled walls, the crytomeria in the garden with views of the bay in gaps between, the bulbous prongs of the stair rail, these things could be counted, on and on. Quantity alone put them beyond Hiroko's reach. Natsuko turned with satisfaction to climb the stairs. They went first to the end of the passage, into her parents' bedroom.

It was the biggest room upstairs, different from the rest of the house, other rooms were entrenched within the foundations. Trees pressed up against their windows. Filtering through the light was as green and mottled as the murky world of a fish tank. But here, in Kazuo and Frances Akazawa's bedroom, light and a panoramic view of Osaka bay streamed in, unhampered. The room appeared to hang suspended, part of the elements and the sky. Clouds moved across the window, pushing treetops down to a few inches above the sill. But, in this room Natsuko always felt apprehensive, fearing any moment it might blow off into the sky.

Hiroko rushed at once to the window. Her arms pushed down hard and straight upon the ledge, a tendon pulled taut inside her wrist.

'What a view. It's wonderful.' Her breath rushed at the glass, adhering to it in a round furry circle. When she stood back it remained there opaque, beneath the greasy mark of her nose.

She turned next to take in the room, and immediately Natsuko tensed. Each object pulled itself up, alert. Natsuko was at once conscious of four dead and shrivelled roses, in a china jug on a bedside table. The black fingers of a pair of gloves, hanging from a drawer of the dressing-table, would not hide themselves, and the mirror irritatingly reflected these things.

Turning her head slowly Hiroko took in everything in turn. Natsuko held her breath, anxious to keep pace. Each object came forward, was scrutinized and receded. Dust covered boxes on top of the wardrobe, a pile of clothes left loosely on the bed, a wastepaper basket overflowing with tissues, slippers kicked into a corner. From the bedside table Hiroko picked up a photograph of Natsuko and her brother Riichi, running hand in hand on a beach. Putting it down she took up one of Kazuo Akazawa, upon the steps of the university. At this she stared much longer.

'She's not tidy, is she?' said Hiroko at last, turning down the corners of her mouth. Wiping a finger over the shoulders of bottles on the dressing-table, she pushed into a group the

14

eyedrops and the vitamins. Then, leaning forward, a hand casually on the dressing-table, she inspected her face in the mirror, patting her hair, moistening her lips. Next she walked to the bed and gave a small tug to straighten the cover. A silky blouse slipped from a pile of clothes lying there. Hiroko just looked at it and with a shrug turned to the cupboard.

But Natsuko still stood at the dressing-table, unable to lift her eyes, feeling more and more uneasy. For, stencilled in light dust on the surface, were the fingermarks of Hiroko's hand. They stared up rawly, branding the room. Natsuko's mind clogged with thoughts of them, stamped on the wood after Hiroko left the room. They would lie there all day and all night until dusted off. Her parents would sleep here, unknowing. The unease grew deeper, for she knew she had been mistaken. Nothing would ever be beyond Hiroko's reach. Just the flick of her eye, or the touch of a finger drew each thing to her. And afterwards they were no longer the same, but filled by her presence and possession.

Trying not to appear anxious Natsuko stepped forward. The bedcover touched her leg, slippery and cool. She saw Hiroko's hand on the cupboard door, turning the handle, opening it. Quickly then, lowering an arm, Natsuko rubbed her jersey covered wrist across the dust, pressing down hard on the fingermarks.

No dirt clung to her sleeve, but upon the dressing-table a great hole was torn in the dust. The fingermarks were gone. Brushing her arm she stepped back, relieved. The light moved with her, shadows of bottles readjusted themselves in the surface of wood. The fingermarks surfaced again, fainter. No longer an open superficial pattern, they now pressed deep into the polish. Whorls and the texture of skin lay ingrained in it, like the paw marks of an animal in wet cement.

Laughter came suddenly then from behind her, coarse as gravel, making her start. Turning quickly, she saw coming towards her, dancing and twitching, her mother's yellow shantung dress. Above it Hiroko's face grimaced and laughed. Immediately Natsuko's stomach contracted in alarm, thinking Hiroko must have pulled on the dress. Then, behind the yellow pleats, she saw the green slither of a skirt, the dress was still on its hanger. Hiroko clutched it to her, an arm across the waist. It hung before her like a limp rag doll.

'One, two, three . . . one two three . . .' Twirling around, Hiroko danced. The yellow dress jiggled, pulled on the hanger right to left. Between the red band of her lips teeth pushed out, a gold crown caught the light. In her open mouth the tongue curled pinkly against the dark hollow of her throat. Humming tunelessly she came towards Natsuko, jerking in spasms from side to side with strange mechanical intensity.

Terrified at such abandonment Natsuko shouted for Hiroko to stop, putting her hands over her eyes. But through cracks between fingers she saw her still coming. Caught up in the lifeless humming and the twitching yellow dress, she took not the slightest notice of Natsuko.

'One, two, three. One, two, three.' She danced on. Natsuko turned and ran to the window. Outside it was snowing. Gauzy flakes flew at the window, stuck for an instant, then dissolved to pinheads of water. Hiroko's turning body brushed her own, throwing her back. She felt the glass, thin and icy beneath the soft stuff of her sweater. Hiroko swelled in the room to bursting point. The walls were exhausted, but could not release her. She danced on, limbs and skirts leaping about her.

At the dressing-table again Hiroko paused, reaching out to the trinket box there, flipping back the lid. A thin tinny music started, notes pinging precisely at staccato intervals. A key in the side of the box turned slowly round and round. In the lid a little ballerina revolved, stiff and netted, like a speared moth. Hiroko pulled out a string of pearls. Clattering against the side of the box they caught briefly around the key, before she swung them over her head. Then, laughing, she was off. Round and round, again and again.

Anticipating the wildness now, Natsuko pushed back against the window. Hiroko whirled past. And for an instant Natsuko saw herself, minute, reflected in the lustre of each small pearl. A pale blob of face, a red smear of jersey, she swung out about Hiroko's neck. Panic filled her then.

'Stop it! Stop it!' she screamed.

Hiroko danced past. The yellow dress touched Natsuko's leg. A fragment of her mother's perfume tore free and floated back.

Then suddenly Hiroko was falling, down upon the bed. The dancing finished, abruptly as it started. Panting and laughing she lay there, the yellow dress spread over her, body sunk deep into the mattress. The satin stripes of the bedcover gathered, broken about her. The beads lay still, flung sideways on to the pillow. Her legs stuck straight out before her, one bent slightly, the other straddling the pile of clothes on the bed, scattering some upon the floor. Between her legs a broad triangle of thigh showed white and blatantly against the green skirt, then darkness.

Natsuko stood by the bed, staring at Hiroko's face glowing up from the blue striped cover, skin stretched taut and smooth over her high flat cheekbones. Her body heaved with sobs of laughter. At that angle her eyes appeared no more than two narrow slits. Within them was blackness, both languid and wild.

'Natsuko. Natsuko.' Frances Akazawa's voice was near, climbing the stairs.

In an instant the room was still, then Hiroko swung from the bed, straightening the cover as she turned. Into the cupboard she quickly shoved the yellow dress. The hanger stuck out awkwardly, a yellow shoulder hitched up high. Forcing the door shut upon it she bent to the fallen clothes, dumping them in a heap on the bed. Then, pushing past Natsuko she stuffed the beads back into the trinket box.

When Frances Akazawa came into the room they stood again together in the frame of the window, silent and watchful. Smiling faintly, Frances pushed the hair off her face with a nervous, restless movement.

'Are you showing Hiroko around? That is good, but now Hiroko must come with me. There are things I must explain to her in the kitchen.'

Natsuko wanted then to cry out, to tell her. But from behind Hiroko took her arm. Through the jersey Natsuko felt nails press into her flesh, pinching hard.

'Come, Hiroko.' Frances Akazawa inclined her head.

Hiroko moved forward, following her out of the door. The room was suddenly silent, the walls breathed, the window loomed up to prominence again. Natsuko was left alone. But on her arm the flesh, released, smarted like a burn.

[2]

It came again as it had the night before, at eleven-thirty. The thin, high wail of a pipe, slicing darkness and silence. She awoke, knowing it had been, listening for it to come again. The notes warbled lightly downwards, mournful over the bay. Then it was there near the house, ending in a sigh. As the note died the sound hung on, amputated, hovering in darkness above her bed. Pulling the warmth of the quilts about her Natsuko pushed down, covering her head. It was difficult to breathe and her ears were still alive, straining and waiting. Drilling into the padding it came again, slipping through the cold night glass of the window to touch her.

Throwing back the covers then, she ran out of the room, down the dark passage. A draught blew up her nightdress between her legs, contracting her skin to goose-pimples. The bare boards of the corridor numbed her feet. It did not help to know it was only the pipe of a noodle cart, wheeling a last round through the streets.

Under Riichi's door was a slither of light. It was always here she ran, when she woke in the night. Not her parents' room, where her father sent her sternly back to bed, sometimes walking her there himself, his pyjamas crumpled, his hair twisted into peaks, his voice firm, tolerating no cowardly thoughts. He never allowed her mother to come: 'No, Frances, I will take her. She must learn.' His voice lumped them together, she and her mother, in an area of inadequacy and self indulgence. But Riichi told nobody and

19

allowed her into the warmth of his bed, if the dreams were too bad.

Wanting to cry out in relief she opened the door and saw Riichi, standing just inside, before a long mirror on the wall, lost in a world of fantasy. He was naked to the waist. Around the top of his underpants he wore the wide knitted stomach warmer their father sometimes used in winter. An unhemmed cotton kitchen cloth, folded to a slim white band, was tied about his head, in the manner of old samurai when they pledged to fight until death. His hands swung high above his head, clutching the long slim body of a sword. Through the knitted belt the bony arc of his diaphragm cut up into his chest.

Afterwards she remembered his arms coming down towards her slowly. But she knew this was only in her mind, for she heard the swish of metal as the sword cut through the air. On her arm its touch was light. She felt nothing but a coldness before the smarting began. Looking down she saw the fine, red line of blood, and seeing shock on Riichi's face, began to cry.

'It's nothing. Only a scratch. Don't cry. You'll wake them all up.' Riichi pulled her to the bed and began wrapping the wound in the cotton headband, winding it tightly round her arm, tucking the end in the top. It was broad and white on her arm, blue printed Chinese characters on it advertised beer. She remembered a delivery boy with crates of bottles handing the cloth over the gate as a customary New Year present. Now, through the prongs of thick square Chinese writing she saw the first smear of blood break through.

'It's nothing. It will dry up in a moment,' Riichi said again. He was sliding the sword back into the scabbard. With a blunt click she heard it lock into place. The sword was the longest of five hanging on the wall in their father's study. The scabbard was glossy and black, antique and valuable. She had never seen it off the wall. Its background was the thick beige slub of the wallpaper, a soiled mark under the supporting bracket. It merged and belonged there. Against the bare flesh of Riichi's thigh the blade looked evil.

'You're not allowed to touch them.' She shivered.

'Father said they'll be mine one day.' His face was suddenly stubborn. He assumed this expression all the time now, since he became seventeen, using it often on his mother. For, against the wishes of Frances Akazawa he now learnt *kendo*, the ancient fencing art. She acquiesced only because in place of a sword, a long slim wooden pole was used. She had a horror of all weapons.

Soon after Riichi started Natsuko had gone one evening with her parents, to the fencing academy to watch. They were impressed by the large hall and the rows of boys, facing each other, in traditional dark blue *kimono* trousers. Meshed faces and hard lacquered breast plates made them look like trousered ants. Frances Akazawa smiled, pointing to Riichi. But when the boys launched into free combat, lunging at each other, stick meeting stick, her expression withdrew. For the hall was then filled with the flailing of sticks, one upon another. A terrible thrashing sound echoing up to the glass roof of the gymnasium, falling down upon them again. It did not stop. Hands over ears, Frances dropped her head to her lap with a moan, her body limp and trembling. They helped her out, one on each side of her, and drove home in silence.

From the back seat Natsuko watched the line of her mother's cheek. Occasionally it flinched as a passing head-light beamed into the car. On her father's face was the same expression she saw when she woke at night, his mouth tight, his eyes intolerant. Only just now it was all carved in much deeper. She sat looking from one profile to the other, the bones and lines, lost in darkness would suddenly flare up in brilliant patches, caught by passing light. Worry made a tight ball in Natsuko's belly. In the car silence was flat and functionless, trampled and bruised about her mother. Once, half way home, Frances turned her face a little, looking at Kazuo.

'I can't help it. It was the noise. I cannot stand a noise like that any longer.' Her voice was pinched and pleading.

But looking ahead over the steering wheel Kazuo only nodded. Silently, Frances examined his impassive profile, and then slumped back.

'I just don't know what is the matter with me any more. Forgive me please.' Her voice was tired, Kazuo nodded again. At home Frances Akazawa went straight to bed.

Now, seeing the sword in Riichi's hand Natsuko remembered her mother's terror, and felt it touch her also. Quickly, she pulled her feet up into Riichi's bed, beneath the thick eiderdown, patterned with stripes and fans. Sometimes, when she came to Riichi's room like this, running down the passage in the dark, he did not even wake, just grunted and turned over. And the warmth, the nearness of his body, the strange male smell of his bed, different from her own, comforted. But now she felt only soreness on her arm, and held it tightly over the bandage. She had intruded, Riichi did not want her here.

'Don't tell anyone.' He threatened, leaning over her on the bed. 'It's only a small scratch. I did not know you would rush in like that.'

Above the beige stomach belt his nipples stared at her

22

reproachfully. Natsuko thought then of the other time he had threatened her with the same words.

It had been three months before, on New Year's Eve. On that day each year their father insisted they go at midnight to the big Shinto shrine in the town. As they approached they heard the drums from streets away, booming rhythmically out. It was past midnight, the gates were already open and two huge bonfires alight in the courtyard. High on the parapet of the ornate roofed gate were the four drums, floodlit. Each had two drummers, naked but for loincloths and short *happi* coats. In the frozen night air they sweated, their skin glazed, attacking the drums again and again.

Flares, bonfires and electric light flooded the shrine. People overflowed up the steps and around the huge bell rope. Pushing their way through the crowd they reached the massive swinging rope, and with both hands shook it in turn, disturbing the bell at the top, rumbling up the gods. They bowed, threw coins in the offering box, and dispatched the gods back by a clapping of hands. Then Kazuo led them to the inner shrine. It was quiet and empty there. Side by side they sat on stools. Behind, through open wooden arches, the crowd was a moving swell, contained by a light barrier. The clink of coins and the dull rattle of the bell played steadily under the beat of drums. In heavy brocade robes a priest purified them by waving a wand of hemp and paper streamers. With a high pitched cry he called down the gods once again, to partake of a ceremonial meal on the altar, of rice cakes, *sake* wine and fruit. Kazuo laid a twig of sacred tree on the altar, and with another cry the gods were sent back.

Between her mother and Riichi, Natsuko waited, for the cup of rice wine the priest would give them at the end. Looking down her nose she watched her breath freeze, tearing away from her into the night. Beside her, on a high pole to the right hung a brocade banner, a long flowing strip of cloth, reaching almost to the ground. It billowed gently in the breeze. She took no notice until the wind, in a sudden rush, blew down between the tall red arches of the shrine. Then the banner writhed about, twisting up to her, touching her gently on the arm once before it dropped back. It blew up again and she saw it, coming flatly at her. The faded, whirling pattern of chrysanthemums in threadbare golds, oranges and greens weaved about before her. Then, with a soft slap, it enveloped her face. On her mouth she tasted metallic thread and the weathered, musty cloth, smelling of incense and rain. As she tugged, trying to free her face, the wind wrapped it tighter about her. It touched the bones beneath her skin, filling her head with icy dreams. She screamed out. And instantly it was gone, dropping away, tamed and quiet in the priest's hand. Shaking his wand of paper bits, he secured it to the pole again. But even after the rice wine, in its shallow red lacquer cup, the taste of old cloth remained on her tongue. The feel of it, mummified about her face, lasted for days. She knew then, no good could come of the year.

Walking down the steps, through the jostling crowds, they reached again the courtyard below. Here shrine shops were open, selling horoscopes, good omens and ornamental arrows of luck. Small trees in the courtyard were decorated by a shower of horoscope predictions, left folded and tied in neat bows among leaves. The trees looked bloated but dignified and festive. The courtyard was brighter than day, blazing with illumination, deep shadows puckering the edges, the sky black and empty above. They stood on the top of more sheer steps, looking down on the narrow streets leading to the shrine. They were lined by stalls draped in red and white bunting, where trinkets, toffee apples, roasted chestnuts, grilled squid and candy floss were sold. There were games to catch goldfish and shoot wooden ducks. Between this lighted border of stalls, was the slow movement of hundreds of heads, like a dark, sluggish river. Above, breath and smoke froze in clouds on the midnight air. There was a smell everywhere of broiled octopus, fish and charcoal.

Leaving their parents at the horoscopes, Natsuko and Riichi went down into it all, hand in hand. First they bought batter cakes in the shape of fish, filled with sweet purple bean paste, then toffee apples. Biting through the cold brittle glaze, crunching it on their teeth, stamping their feet to keep warm, they walked on. It had begun to snow. Looking up into the black hole of sky Natsuko saw the flakes, lighted from below, spinning down upon them like feathers emptied from a bag.

It was then they found the marquee. It was erected triangularly, across the corner of a parking lot, backed by a wall. Above the tent large pictures in magenta, blue and green showed the elongated white faces and enormous wigs of *geisha* women, in the manner of old woodblock prints. Stuck across paltry wooden slats the thin paper bulged with the breeze, in places the faces were ripped open. Spilling from a generator box, wire coiled over the pavement to two arc lamps, blazing either side of the tent. Near the entrance a short fat man in a red ski jacket, shouted into the microphone, announcing the next performance. People disgorged through the flap of the tent from the last show, a smell of beer breaking from them. A man turned to the wall beside Natsuko, to urinate. A liquid arc spurted from him, the warmth of it rising in steam. He turned and she saw him then, hard and straight as a stick between the buttons.

Pulling her with him, Riichi walked round to the side of the tent. Against the wall there, high up, was a slim gap in the canvas that Riichi was tall enough to look through. Pressing his knee to the wall, his foot resting on a rough crack, he pulled Natsuko up on to his leg. Half clinging to the top of the wall, half sitting on Riichi's knee, she was able to see through the slit.

The view was not clear, they were behind tiered stands of seats. At first ankles and shoes were all she saw. Then, in gaps between trouser legs, appeared part of a rough wooden stage, raised up high on stilts. On the ground below were the painted white lines of parking spaces. A woman knelt at the side of the stage, grey haired and dressed in a sombre patterned *kimono*. With a white paddle-shaped plectrum she was twanging the strings of a *samisen*, held upon her lap. At the first pause another woman came out on to the stage, standing still and posed at the centre. She was the long white face outside, on the pictures above the tent ripped by the wind, the same tiny eyes, the pagoda of hair. She was the face Natsuko remembered in her grandmother's house, from old *Kabuki* programmes stored in a trunk and looked over on rainy days. At home she stared out of old prints and her father's scholarly books, bathing, loving, collecting fireflies and powdering her neck. Now, on the creaking stage above white parking lines, she began to dance. Slowly, sedately, her limbs moved, her body turned. The greens and reds of her *kimono* dipped and swayed. At the back of her neck it dropped low, showing a white fall of skin. The stiff lacquered coils and loops of the wig were twisted with bands of silk, stuck with red pins and hanging silver ornaments. Below her face was a floury white, half erasing her lips to a bright tiny bud. The *samisen* twanged, she raised an arm, the long

26

sleeves swung as she moved precisely across the stage and back.

Sitting on Riichi's knee, Natsuko no longer felt the wind chilling the side of her face, or the narrow discomfort of Riichi's thigh. The past, dead among mothballs and old paper, took on new shape. She sat forward, intense.

But the face, bland and stately until now, began to crack open. A coarse smile filled the white paint. The movement of the hands had suddenly nothing to do with the rhythm of the *samisen*. They were pulling awkwardly at the stiff folds of the *obi* sash. Natsuko saw it begin to untie, rolling away like string from a parcel, as the woman pulled it from her, yard after yard. It dropped and lay on the stage, stretched out in a crumpled, goldworked snake. She danced on, her face splintering lewdly. Her eyes rolled, her tongue licked her lips, sneaky and hungry. And suddenly the *kimono* dropped, a soft gaudy mass at her feet. After it, one by one, the under *kimono* fell in pastel heaps, almond, white and pink. The last was pink again, and Natsuko saw there was nothing more. The woman stood still a moment, a slit of skin to her waist, a swell of breast beneath. Then, slowly, she withdrew her arms, until the top slipped down about the tie at her waist. A rustle spread through the tent. On the wooden stands feet uncrossed and recrossed.

The pictures of old prints were lost, the *Kabuki* programmes gone. In her stomach Natsuko felt a quickening. But the breasts were disappointing, not the expected fleshiness, just flat, with a boniness across the top. The woman moved nearer, and Natsuko saw goose-pimples on her upper arms. In the cold her nipples were contracted and small, the skin puckered tightly about them. She grinned again, her mouth gold-filled and hideous.

Overwhelmingly then it repulsed her. Curiosity gone, it

was only grotesque and horrible. The thin, uninteresting body, and above it the head, huge, black and artificial. It was the head of a fly she had once seen magnified, shiny and bulbously coiled. Behind, where the woman's neck joined her back, three long points of white paint divorced it from the flesh below. The music twanged on, Natsuko waited, knowing what was to come.

But Riichi lowered his knee then, forgetting her, and she slipped, falling awkwardly to the pavement. He was standing right up against the canvas now, under his jeans the muscle of his thigh was hard and tense. She pulled at his jacket, but his body was fixed, he took no notice of her. She leaned back against the wall and waited, feeling unnecessary and small. Her bare fingers hurt with cold, she retrieved her gloves from the pocket of her coat, and pulled them on. Inside the tent the *samisen* twanged. The notes came to her, separate and slightly off key. Then abruptly they stopped. And beside her Riichi took a sharp breath, like a sob.

Afterwards he took her fiercely by the shoulders and said, 'Don't tell anyone.'

Now she felt the same angry feeling warm in her as on that New Year's Eve. Pushing down and away from Riichi she buried under his quilt, hating the soreness on her arm, and the discomfort of anger in her throat. Suddenly there were wide spaces, silence and uncertainty. She could no longer be sure about Riichi. He seemed to be slipping away down a long tunnel. His outline was no longer clear. He said and did things now that fitted no known context. She was sure only of being alone, where Riichi had stood with her before. But she promised as she had the other time, for he could still intimidate her.

28

'No. I won't tell.'

Turning her eyes away she looked beyond the flat nipples of his chest, under his armpit with its soft, new hair, across the sea of stripes and fans. She saw it then, in a corner of the room, sitting on the floor below the window. The worn toy bear of Riichi's, that she too had played with. It was slashed in the face, through the black wool of its nose. Frayed and parted strands stood up, like whiskers around the bald open tip. And below, its belly was all cut about. White stuffing spewed out in a solid lump. Fear started up inside her then.

Seeing her looking at the bear Riichi, saying nothing, took a paper bag from the drawer of his desk. Tipping out the few matchboxes it contained, he stuffed the bear inside. Silently he rolled it up and pushed it into the wastepaper basket. But under the paper, the bulge of its head peered over the top. Putting out the light, he got into bed.

Suddenly then, Natsuko did not want to stay, and ran back again into the room. It was silent, the pipe gone. She tucked down deeply in bed. On her arm Riichi's bandage moved against the soreness. She knew she would not sleep. In the dark well beneath the covers, she saw again the white mound of stuffing against the belly of the bear. And on her arm was the constant smarting of the thin sliced line through her flesh. She lay staring at the ceiling, hovering darkly above, and prayed for sleep.

Standing beside the breakfast table, Frances Akazawa stopped talking as Hiroko knocked. Coming in with a tray of tea, Hiroko placed it on the table, and gave a small bow to Kazuo sitting there. He returned a curt nod, but noticed the thick fold of lid against her cheek, and her neck, smooth inside the collar of her blouse. As she left Frances began to speak again.

'I insist it is to be kept in the study, upon the wall. It is not to be touched. It is a dangerous weapon. You know how I feel about such things.' She faced Kazuo squarely.

Stretching out calmly, he took a slice of toast from the plate, and Frances' voice rose sharply on the last words. Natsuko stood behind her mother. It had been impossible to hide the scratch. Although not deep it had needed some attention.

'That sword is too old to be sharp. Besides he is a boy. You know you take the wrong attitude to things here. I was brought up to understand the responsibilities of being a man.' Kazuo buttered toast, and refused to look up. Beside him at the table Riichi stared at his hands.

'I've told you before, I no longer care about what you consider right or wrong. I've tried all these years to understand, you know that. But it's all back to front as far as I can see. It's unethical and horrible deliberately to direct a child's mind to things of violence, and at so young an age. I cannot bear it. I cannot take any more of anything here. And God knows, I've tried.' Her voice rose to a strident squeak.

Holding her mother's hand, Natsuko kept her eyes on the carpet. Anxiety twisted inside her. It was always like this, her mother hysterical, her body tense and hard, throwing words before her like chipped stones. And her father, impenetrable, holding his stance until her mother became soft and tearful. She hated it all. She held tighter to her hand and concentrated on pale flecks of wool in her mother's skirt that surfaced in little pebbles the colour of wet sand. Clenched about Natsuko, Frances' hand showed a whitening across the knuckles and the outer rim of nail.

'There is nothing wrong as far as I can see. You're just getting hysterical.' Kazuo spread marmalade upon the toast. Natsuko watched it mix with the melted butter.

'But he might have killed Natsuko. Who knows what all this may lead to. I will not have it. Do you understand? I cannot bear any more. You just don't care about my feelings.' She pulled her hand free of Natsuko, and as she sobbed the pleats of the sandy skirt moved lightly.

At the table Riichi looked questioningly at his father. Frances' sobs filled the room, bitterness congealed in her face. Kazuo looked at her, pursing his lips, a muscle throbbing below his cheek. He turned to Riichi.

'Do not take it again from the study.' The words spat from him harshly.

'Are you satisfied now?' Kazuo threw the sentence at Frances, hard and flat. It clattered in pieces about them all.

Riichi looked at Natsuko, his eyes bit into her. And she knew then she was not mistaken, there was a difference in Riichi. It had begun on New Year's Eve. Nothing she might say could define it clearly. But Riichi had changed. The difference was something inside him, something she could not see. She looked at the four of them then, and saw the dark feeling crashing between them. She clutched tighter at her mother's skirt and sobbed with fear and consternation.

In their bedroom that night, Kazuo tried again. The quilt was pulled high about Frances' shoulders, she lay with her back to him. Under the covers he moved his arm, until his hand rested across her belly.

'You should not feel as you do. You have lived here so long now. You should be over those kind of feelings. You understand the culture. Wherever I can I have adapted to your ways and ideas, more than most men here would. But there are things Riichi must learn, from my side as well as yours.' He said it gently, meaning it. Pushing down the blankets a little he moved his hand up, cupping her breast. Immediately she tensed.

'No. Please. Not now.' She pulled away.

'For God's sake, Frances, what more do you want me to do? Do I consciously behave in the way other Japanese husbands do? How many times have I gone out, after work before I come home, to a bar, as most of my colleagues do? They think me an oddity. In the beginning they made fun of me. I never told you, but I've put up with a lot for your sake.'

But of course he loved her. They had married in the Western sense, and their relationship was on quite a different footing from those of his friends. He had studied and lived abroad. He knew very well all Frances' theories and ideals. But he wished she would stop fighting the society in which they now lived. He wished she would sympathize with the Japanese point of view, and leave it at that. But she refused to accept that a consistent attitude to living was simply not expected. Every sphere of life, every situation and each age had its own code of behaviour. Each day was filled by contradictions, man must be allowed the disguises of the chameleon, to adapt to each. Complications resulted if these different spheres and their codes of behaviour were mixed. But Frances would not have it.

She had not got over his father keeping a mistress. He knew, secretly, she lived with the fear of him doing the same. Her horror had never subsided at the discovery that the bills for his father's philandering nights came home to his wife to pay. Yet Kazuo, in his childhood, accepted that the province of wife was entirely fenced off from the province of erotic pleasure, that each sphere was equally open and above-board that each gracefully accepted the other. His mother had sometimes dropped remarks that made him realize she was not entirely happy with this state of affairs. But she was always cool and dignified, helping his father dress for his evenings, tending him when he came home in a drunken state. She knew her place.

Once, he had seen his father's mistress. It was the day his grandmother had taken him to see the *Kabuki*. It was the season of the *Kaomise* in Kyoto. All the best people went there. It was the first day, the *geisha* were turned out in force with their patrons. His grandmother was very annoyed they had only been able to obtain seats at the back of the stalls. But Kazuo was small and impressed by it all. And in those days it had been gracious and lavish. The audience was not the crowd they were now, with their casual clothes, cheap disposable lunch boxes, and throw-away plastic pitchers of green tea. Then it was silk and brocade and pinstriped suits, many of the men still wore *kimono*. Lunch was served from tiers of painted lacquer boxes, the tea was in china bowls. He never knew if his grandmother even saw his father there. She did not take note of things she did not wish to see.

There was a tall pile of the painted lacquer boxes balanced on the knee of the woman beside his father. She handled them deftly, serving delicacies of every sort. She was young and pretty, much prettier than Kazuo's mother. But her manner did not seem as cool and dignified, and Kazuo noticed at the neck the *kimono* dipped to an immodest low. And even from their seats he could feel, below the propriety of public behaviour, an informality. His father would sometimes lean towards the woman, or she would laugh coyly behind her hand, after giving his father a little push. Kazuo had always observed a great display of formality between his

33

parents. Even within the most intimate circle of family life he had not once seen an erotically affectionate gesture. From the back of the stalls Kazuo had watched intently. It was clear the relationship here was very different from the one his father had with his mother. But he did not remember feeling outraged, only intrigued, and underneath in some way profoundly excited.

He looked at Frances' sullen back now with cold resentment. It was always the same. Even those times she acquiesced left them sour. He turned and let her alone, resentful and unwilling to coax. She huddled deeper beneath the covers, back to him, knees drawn up, her hair spread lankly behind her on the pillow.

It had irretrievably fallen apart. He could see that. She had lost the will to go on. He no longer knew how to try. Because he understood something of the difficulties she faced, of custom and culture, they had moved from his parents' home as the children began to grow. They came here, to this large, tense Western-style house on a hillside above Kobe. He found it too upright in every way. But it was what Frances wanted. Yet, even after they moved, nothing seemed to please her. He watched bitterness grow inside her, sapping her body until it was stringy. He remembered the very abundance of her that had first attracted him. The swingy walk, the smile, the way of flicking her hair. Now flesh hung upon her in a disappointed way, her limbs showed sinew, her neck was thin and taut, held for years in a defensive position. At times he felt guilty, knowing he could not meet her expectations. Even the thought of trying tired him. Sometimes he was certain of the mistake, to have ever brought her here. Then again it seemed her own doing, for she should have adapted, have made more effort, he said to himself. Instead, growing older, she clung the more impassively to her own opinions and ideas. She said she must retain her identity. He was tired of it all.

Stretching out he switched off the light and settled down, his back still to Frances. And for a moment the woman, Hiroko, came into his mind. He saw again the thick, lazy fold of lid against the cheek. He knew the kind of woman she was; Frances had not judged wrongly. She would give anyone whatever they wanted. She would do anything. Anything.

[3]

It was not the first time. Once before it had happened. Somebody brought her home in a taxi from a department store in Kobe, after she collapsed at the bottom of an escalator, sobbing. In the first aid room they got no sense from her. That time a shopgirl brought her home. The doctor, when he came, found little wrong, prescribed a tranquillizer and a day in bed.

It was a phone call this time, from a pinball arcade. The telephone number had been found on a card in her handbag. In his study Kazuo Akazawa laid down the article he was writing for an American magazine on *Bushido*, the old samurai ethical code, and drove into town to fetch her.

Sitting in a small pale blue rocking chair by the window in her bedroom, Natsuko listened to the hysterical sobbing in her parents' bedroom. On her lap she pulled at the dry blonde hair of a doll, hating its matted texture that could never be combed. As it rocked gently on her lap its eyelids lifted lazily a fraction, and closed, over and over again. Angry suddenly at its unbreakable face, she began moving frantically in the chair, the muscles of her body hard and tense, pushing back and forth. And the eyes on her lap snapped open and shut with a light clicking sound, the glassed velvet of the iris stricken and wide. Hoarse and splintered, in the next room the sobbing went on. Outside the sky was pale and flat, without cloud or colour. The bare branches of a willow tree unravelled like tangled wire. She wished she did not feel compelled to sit as she did, listening, waiting.

She knew her mother went to those places, playing the pinball machines for hours. Once Natsuko went with her, and could not understand what kept her there. Until that day she had only seen the pinball arcades from outside, hating the gaudy lights and raucous noise.

She remembered there were three of the places, one after another, taking up most of the block, all rooted under massive, garish film hoardings. Thinking of the fencing academy she wondered why the noise did not affect her mother. For even on the pavement outside the glass doors, the loud metallic moan pushed out. And the sheer thunder of it all inside, had terrified Natsuko. Wild bumping balls, rattling, rolling, pinging through holes in row after row of machines, and above it all piped rock music, blaring away. As soon as they opened the door it engulfed her at once with splendour, intense and trivial. Lights winked from machines and raced, blinking on and off, in a constant chase around the walls. Across the ceiling were massed fairy lights and boughs of shiny, plastic red maple leaves. For then it had been Autumn, maple viewing time in the shrines and hills. But her mother sat there, before a blue machine, fixed and dead to Natsuko's presence. In the window of the thing a brightly painted face grinned out, wide, toothy mouth, popping eyes, red cheeks, a little black hat with a purple feather. Holes filled the eye pupils, the nostrils and missing teeth. While the machine was in use the head bobbed cheekily up and down. In a corner of the frame was a hand with a gun, and from outside a lever pinged bullets at the head. Natsuko saw not just one, but a whole row of identical machines, with identical heads, hands and guns. All the way

37

down the row the moronic grins and little hats with purple feathers bobbed up and down, defiant. Natsuko hated the noise, the sight of it all, and the feeling of aimless despair. In this pulsating cell everything disintegrated. All the darkness of past and future receded and, in its cessation, lost hopes roller-coasted the silver balls until they burst in jackpots and laughter. On a stool beside her mother Natsuko prayed for it all to stop, if only for a moment. The continual roar, the speeding walls, the scraping of chairs on the concrete floor, and a terrible smell of cesspools and orange juice.

On the next machine to them was a man with a head of cropped bristles, the pale skin of his skull showing through beneath. He wore a gaudy, Hawaian shirt under a stomach warmer, and on his bare feet wooden Japanese clogs, with stilted ridges several inches high. She knew he was a gangster. Riichi was always pointing them out. They looked like that. He focused a wide derisive grin at them. It was then she noticed other people staring at them also. When they were not concentrating on the machines women giggled, men laughed openly. She was sure they made rude jokes about them. Fear and revulsion jostled in her, at the incongruity of her mother in this place. But Frances seemed oblivious.

She sat, pulling the lever, pressing coins into the slot, firing again and again. From the blue frame the face grinned out, its neck a thin white stick. Mostly the balls just pinged the blank areas of cheek and forehead, but once or twice they shot through the holes and fell with a hard plop the other side of the head. Then a red light flashed on top of the machine, a bell rang and a handful of discs fell into a metal cup. These Frances could exchange for cigarettes, sweets or a variety of prizes.

As the discs spilt out, clinking into the metal cup Frances

turned and smiled at Natsuko, reaching out, squeezing her arm. Natsuko was apprehensive. At home her mother did not smile, her face was always shuttered. Now, scooping up discs, her eyes were bright, her expression determined. She pushed the discs into her pocket and Natsuko thought, now it must end, now it must finish. She stood up to leave, but Frances was pulling again at the machine.

Desperation came down upon Natsuko then. The noise grew uncontained around her. She tugged at Frances' arm, beginning to cry. Her mother stood up reluctantly at last, and they left the dreadful place.

Outside, sun cut through the narrow spaces between tall buildings, splashing the jumble of advertisements, windows, traffic and people. To Natsuko this was serene after the world inside the pinball arcade. Yet her mother stood in a dazed way in the street, and seemed not to know which way to go, her face tight and blank again. In the end Natsuko had taken her hand and walked towards the bus stop.

'But why? Why must you go to places like that? And what for?' Kazuo sat on the side of the bed, leaning over Frances. Although he tried, her swollen face aroused only a guilty disgust in him. He hoped nobody who knew them had ever seen her go in or out of the place. It was a shock to learn she went there.

'I've only been sometimes, when I felt too bad.' Her voice was thick and nasal.

'But why?' He could not help the raised tone of his voice, the cold exasperation. He felt he had endured enough.

'I don't know. The feeling I might win . . .' Beneath the sobs her eyes were timid, refusing to look at him.

'But there is little money to it.' He was glad she was afraid, maybe ashamed. Suddenly he hated her so much, he just wanted to shake her and shake her, until her body fell apart, and he would be left alone, in peace, without her at last.

'Not in that way . . . oh . . . you would never understand. Everything stops there, only the moment you stand in exists . . . and ahead, anything is possible, even a jackpot. And it's me . . . me who can do it. How could you ever understand? You get everything you want, it all goes your way . . . nothing in life evades you, you would never understand!'

'No. I don't. What happened to you there?' he said sharply, afraid suddenly of the fierceness inside him.

'I don't know. I can't remember.' The sobbing started again.

'You must remember.'

'Yes . . . I couldn't do it right. Nothing came. It wouldn't give a damn thing. God, I was angry. Angry.' She screamed the words out, her head thrashing the pillow, sobs gushing up from her again.

'All right. All right.' It frightened him, this hysteria. It aggravated his anger, making him afraid he really might lash out and hit or choke her. He patted her arm, trying to calm them both. The words were entangled in sobs now, falling freely from her. He had to listen hard to understand.

'Then they started laughing at me. I could feel them, hear them. Everyone was laughing at me. And the noise of it got louder and louder. All of it. The music, the machines, the laughter. Everything. It was terrible. I thought it would crack my head. Then I don't remember anything until you came.'

She took off her shoes, they told him, hitting the machine again and again with the heels, flailing at it with hands and feet, screaming and sobbing. They were on the verge of calling the police when they found the telephone number in her bag.

The noise, the lights, the thick human smell of the place had punched his senses. The rows of glazed eyes made him feel sick, as did the sight of Frances kneeling huddled and sobbing on the floor. He smarted at having to own her. But she had come with him easily enough, suddenly quietened and dazed at the sight of him.

Now, exhausted and blotched, her face stared up at him from the pillow. Mascara blurred her eyes, making them round and black and ghoulish. Tears rolled into her hair, soaking the temples, pasting the strands together. He felt only disgust at the sight of her, and pity for himself. Standing up he walked to the telephone. She needed a doctor. He knew now she was ill.

From the window in her parents' bedroom Natsuko watched the next day. Frances and Kazuo bent under the twisted fir tree arched over the gate, going to the hospital. Only from this window was the view clear, of the garden, the gate and the hill beyond. But she hesitated to come into the room alone, knowing she would feel Hiroko here, see her spread out on the bed again, the yellow dress across her, the wild eyes and open mouth staring up from her body.

Even from that distance it was clear something was gone from her mother's body. It was limp. Leaning heavily upon Kazuo's arm, her head drooped near his shoulder, but did not rest upon it. Natsuko watched them disappear gradually, down the steep flight of steps in front of the house. Abruptly the pale fan of hair over her mother's fur collar vanished. The top step welled up, empty. A car door slammed, the engine whirred. For a brief moment sun glinted on the roof of the car as it slid down the hill. They were gone. But Natsuko continued to stand by the window, looking.

Empty land before the house slipped away sharply in a verge of yellow winter grass. Marking the road, telephone poles sank at a perpendicular angle. Diminished and far below, the heavy tiled roofs of a Zen monastery stood out, in its garden a pale clump of nine bamboos. Below that again spread the texture of the town, the chimneys of the steel works, and the sea of Osaka bay. The sombre reflections of clouds moved quickly over its surface.

Grey ribbons cut through the town, and upon them traffic moved as small black blobs. Ships pushed slowly between the cranes and jetties of the harbour. Chimneys smoked. A train rushed forward towards Osaka, a dusty snake of indeterminate colour. Things happened there in the town, each moment something moved, bursting into sound or action. Mechanical cause produced mechanical effect. It was all quick, orderly and foreseeable.

But here, up the steep mountainside above the town, it was as if a giant hand had torn away the land beneath them. Cut off by silence and space they alone seemed to hang here, precipitously. Shrouded by mists the movement of birds and the sloughing of wind through trees and grass was the only life. Natsuko did not trust it here, feeling from the beginning vulnerable.

Before they had lived with her father's parents, in an old Japanese house, in Japanese style. For how long they were there she did not know, for she had been very small. Then they moved here, to this house, and afterwards the grandparents died, one following the other rapidly. In their house her mother had found it impossible to live; she was always crying.

Natsuko remembered little. Only hazy edged images slipped through her mind, their memories unconnected. Preceding her up slippery narrow stairs she saw the white *tabi* socked feet of her grandmother, shuffling pigeon-toed, below the hem of a grey *kimono*. Somewhere upstairs were decorated paper boxes, stacked one on top of another, and a tall red lacquer chest. In them were stored her grandmother's *kimono*. Sometimes Natsuko had been allowed to look. Then, pressing her fingers into the soft cool silks she touched outlines of clouds and birds. The room was dim, the matted floor tight, but she remembered there only a gentle coloured sea of peonies, willows and wild ginger leaves.

In that house she and Riichi slept on *futon* on the floor, although her parents had a bed. Lying on those quilts she remembered the low smooth eye levels, the feeling of space. From the matted *tatami* floor near her face came an astringent smell. The rush mats were padded, fitted one into another like a puzzle. The woven sheen of them, polished by morning light, was the first thing she saw when she woke. The bean-filled pillows had white frilled coverlets, and through the cloth she pressed the small lumps between her fingers. The beans inside made a sighing noise when she turned the pillow over. The kitchen had been brown wood with warm piquant smells, jars of fermenting pickles, sour and strong, roasted rice cakes that pulled like rubber on her teeth. She remembered a vase of first chrysanthemums, smelling of Autumn and the sadness of the hills. The shadow of bamboo leaves on a paper door, and the sound of rain, dripping through trees on to the moss-covered stones of the garden. In that rain her grandmother wore special pink plastic toecaps over her wedged sandals and white *tabi* socks. And each Summer was carried upon her beige linen parasol, bobbing like a jerky dragon-fly.

Clearly in Natsuko's memory was the garden, and her grandfather's love of it. When the wide sliding doors of the house were drawn back it came almost into the room. Natsuko had knelt with him on the polished platform of the veranda, while he pruned small potted plants and *bonsai* trees. The garden had not been level. In her mind she saw it gathered at the centre into a mossy green mound, studded with rocks and a small fir tree, the trunk bent and stubby. Above, the branches fanned out in a wide umbrella, supported from below by tall straddled logs, and wire coiled along the branches. Behind a creeper-covered wall set off a whole bed of Chinese bellflowers.

She remembered a pond, not large, but enough for two red and white carp. Beside it she lay on her stomach, looking down through the green water to the soft muddy bottom of rotted leaves. Around the sides ferny weeds waved gently, stirred by the motion of the fish, gauzy tails fanning out behind meandering bodies. Undisturbed she could lie for hours, staring into the water, wishing she too had been born a fish, sealed into the still green world.

Then they moved here. She hated the straight cold house, thin looking on the outside, inside filled with gloomy depth, brown wood and watching passages. It was August. Within three days there had been a typhoon. She had known others, but they were different. Tucked between close neighbours in the town, the grandparents' house had only a small patch of sky above the garden, hemmed in by dark trees and much bamboo. But from this very window in her parents' room, she had watched the vast sky that day, uncontained before her. Far away across the bay the horizon was lost in thick haze, as it had been since the day they arrived. It looked like open sea before them. To the left it stretched as far as she could see, to the smoking factories and gasometers of Osaka, and to the right over Kobe port, to the indistinct outline of Awaji island. Between these two points the clouds rushed bruised and bulbous, mad chariots racing through the sky. Ships left port to anchor in the safety of the bay, hundreds of them dotting the water, rocking on its choppy surface. In the garden wind cut through the heat, rustling leaves with the sound of taffeta, hissing through the tall pampas grass on the slope beyond the gate. Then, slapping the windows in sheets, the rain came suddenly, washing down the stone path and trees until colours deepened and dripped. She had been terrified seeing it all, blowing off the horizon in a bar, like an army advancing towards them. And they, exposed, without defence. In the house they laughed at her. The eye is far away. It is nothing. We will only have side winds, they told her. They played music and made hot drinks, her father had a holiday from the university. But Natsuko sat here, at this window, and watched all that anger blowing at her. Once they persuaded her away, to watch the typhoon news on the television. A yellow map of Japan in a blue sea filled the screen. Upon it the typhoon was an orderly design of circles and lines. A man tapped it briskly with a cane. But returning to the window she wondered where they fitted, all those thin black lines and circles, into the wild sea and the rain. She thought then of a film she had seen, about a girl who visited strange faraway places, flying there upon a magic brass-railed bed. Wind blew out her hair in streamers, filled the puffed sleeves of her nightgown. Clouds rolled by near enough to touch, enveloping her sometimes in mist. It was terrifying. For nights Natsuko slept badly, praying her own

45

bed would not act so strangely. Now, facing the open sky at the window, she felt that fear again.

Gradually it went, hours later. The bay came into focus, exhausted, but clear again. Bordering it the colours of the town were deeper than she had ever seen, each small cell standing out exact and separate. Suddenly then, the other side of the bay, the whole peninsula of Wakayama loomed up to face her, dark and near. Mountains were purple and ridged, the town small white clustered dots along the fore-shore. She drew a sharp breath, for it shocked her more than any moment of the typhoon. It was the sheer deception. Hidden behind a curtain of haze she had not imagined all the time this was there, solid and hard. She had thought they faced open sea.

This room was filled always with the uneasy residue of that day. The window was disconcerting. Blandly flaunting open sky and Wakayama neatly hidden, it continually lied, unrepentant. It frightened her to be here alone. She felt the emptiness of the sky. Looking up, its hollowness never ended, each thin strata gave way to more nothingness. She wondered where it ever ended, and knew herself small, smaller than an ant. Useless and disposable.

[4]

She could see no reason for Hiroko to come to the hospital. Worse still, she made an occasion of it, changing from a green skirt into a *kimono*. Natsuko sat on the matted floor of Hiroko's room and watched her winding the stiff sash of *obi*, round and round her midriff. Through her mind passed a picture of the other *obi*, its crumpled trail lying on the rough boards of the stage. Hiroko finished it neatly, the folds at the back tucked into a small flap. Natsuko wondered where all the cloth had gone. From a band securing the *obi* a toggle hung down, a pitted stone of blue and purple. The greys and mauve of the winter *kimono* blended into the rain-filled sky of the window. The room was warm and stuffy. Below red-hot wire mesh the wick of an oil stove burnt in a blue circle. The scent of cosmetics mixed with its fumes. Hiroko patted powder on to her cheeks, kneeling before a low, mirrored toilet box. She looked neater than in Western clothes, like a parcel, wrapped and tied. But all the fussing and changing only confirmed to Natsuko the fear inside her: that her mother was in a hospital room, shuttered away, attended by doctors and mystery.

'Is she better? Shall we bring her home today?' She expected no assurance from Hiroko, wished she did not find it necessary to ask the question. Nobody would explain what was wrong. In cold, black pockets of the night she feared her mother had died.

Hiroko ran a lipstick over her mouth, rubbing her lips wetly together. Natsuko watched the contortion of her face in

47

the small oval mirror. It reflected the wall behind them, and Hiroko's green skirt, hanging from a hook. Below was a pile of folded quilts, and on top of them the box of biscuits they would take to the hospital. It was done up in a purple carrying cloth, the ends knotted, sticking up above the box like a winged insect.

'She'll never be better, as long as she lives in Japan. That's what they say. None of the foreigners can live here. Sooner or later they all have to go home,' Hiroko said with satisfaction, scrutinizing herself in the mirror, rubbing her lips together again. She never wasted words.

Behind her Natsuko stared down at the upturned soles of Hiroko's feet protruding, neatly socked, from under the tight curve of her buttocks. She glimpsed a portion of leg between the white *tabi* sock and the *kimono* hem, as uncompromising as Hiroko's face.

'They'll send her home to England. That's what your father said.' From a little red pot Hiroko rouged her cheeks.

All the way, from the moment they entered the hospital, along the many corridors, she was conscious of Hiroko. Why must she come, she thought again and again. She disliked Hiroko carrying her mother's favourite biscuits. She or Riichi should have carried them. Instead they swung from Hiroko's fingers as her wedged slippers squeaked over the rubbery floor. Without turning Natsuko saw in her mind the small tripping steps, slightly pigeon-toed. Walking quickly she hoped to outpace Hiroko so that the sound of her feet would be lost. But they still kept rigidly to procession; Natsuko just behind her father, then Riichi and some way back Hiroko.

Frances Akazawa was not in bed. She sat in a chair by the

window. The room was warm, but colourless. Even the metal rim of the bed and the cabinet beside it were painted white. All the darkness was outside the window, upon the wet roofs of the town, and grey banks of swollen cloud.

She turned her face towards them, trying to smile, but only the corners of her mouth twitched slightly. The whiteness of her frightened Natsuko. Her face slipped sometimes into the beige dressing-gown, sometimes into the putty-coloured curtains behind her, stiff and closed. About Natsuko her arms were loose and heavy, the kiss dry. Crowding into the small room they seemed immediately too many, clumsy and vivid. They filled the room with smells of damp cloth and robust colour. Standing awkwardly, sitting upon the high bed and visitors' chairs, they were too much for Frances Akazawa. She began to cry, quietly. Silent tears squeezed from her, running thinly down her cheeks, dripping to the box on her lap, patterning the purple cloth with small, deep spots. Not knowing what to do they stood about uneasily, patting her shoulders. With the tears there was no sound but the odd, harsh intake of breath. That noiselessness was more terrible to Natsuko than any amount of sobbing. It broke out inside her like razor blades, flicking through her veins.

Hiroko had not come into the room. Natsuko saw her standing against the wall outside as the American nun came in. The door closed again, shutting her out. Against its whiteness now stood the nun, tall, the black spectacles on her nose definite within the blankness of her veil and gown.

'Now what is this, Mrs Akazawa? They have all come to see you and you cry. That will not do.' She looked meaningly at Kazuo. He turned to the children.

'Go out now, both of you. Wait with Hiroko.'

Like the room the corridor was pale and warm. The

49

polished floor stretched away either side of Natsuko, reflecting ceiling lights. After the thin, white face of her mother Hiroko looked indestructible. Her mouth stood out, a bright glossy spot. Natsuko could not look. She turned her back and gazed from the window. It had stopped raining. Outside a grassy slope faced her, a sodden dirty yellow. High up, well behind it she saw the corner of a Buddhist cemetery. In the monochrome of path, stone and leafless tree, a polished granite block stood out, wet and shiny as black ice. Quickly she turned to face the corridor again.

Windows lined most of one wall, opposite them a row of identical white doors. Beside each the black printed name of their inmate was slotted. On some notices were pinned: 'No Visitors. No Meals. Operation Schedule.' On her mother's door 'No Visitors' dangled on a blue ribbon. Before these marked doors vases of flowers stood, ominously rejected from inside. There was a smell everywhere of calm bustle, warmth and disinfectant. It was a mission hospital, run by foreign nuns. Natsuko had been born here, Riichi too. The nuns always greeted them kindly, remarking on the growth of their former babies.

The door opened, Kazuo and the nun emerged. They turned to the right and walked silently a short distance down the corridor, then stopped. They stood closely, concern pulling their expressions. The nun placed a hand briefly on Kazuo's arm. Seeping from them words were indistinct. Lacking beginnings or ends, remnants of sentences floated to Natsuko. Reaching out she snapped off a leaf from a cyclamen plant, pressing it over the ball of her thumb. A thin green juice smeared her fingers.

'... but a difficult age ... all these years cut off ... isolation ... consider ... alienated ... and chronic depression . . . oh yes . . . no doubt . . . eventually even a loss of reality . . . then . . .'

Natsuko did not understand the words, but she knew the meanings. And a day at the beginning of Autumn came back to her then. She had gone with her mother to the club in town, to a meeting there of a social group, for the foreign wives of the Japanese. They met in the library, a small sunny room at the back of the club. Natsuko sat beside her mother in a round armchair. From a window behind sun streamed directly on to her neck, there was a smell off the curtains of long hung dust. The women relaxed in a wide circle, their faces bright, their clothes casually special and pressed. First one or two women addressed the group, introducing a new-comer, giving information of products and services. They spoke little of themselves individually, saying more often 'we', with reference to *our special problems*.

Then a grey-haired, large-busted woman called Janet Okuda stood up and talked about the changes she had seen in forty-eight years. When she first arrived in Japan as a new bride, she had been forced to use the back door of the com-munal family house, with other women and servants. Her husband, the eldest son, used the front door with the men. Loudly and gaily Janet Okuda asked the younger women to look at her, to see how well she had survived this and much more. She begged the women to realize what an easy time a young bride now had of it, how cottage cheese, large size tights and ovenproof dishes were now available. How fash-ions no longer took three years to come but were flown red hot from Paris to Tokyo. Christian Dior handbags and Cardin shirts were now the ambition if not the property of every little office girl. And she herself now taught these young women of marriageable age Western etiquette so that,

51

if ever they accompanied a prospective husband abroad a foreign menu or more might not floor them. They, the foreign wives of the Japanese, were now at a clear advantage, said Janet Okuda. It was no more like it used to be. Isolation was obsolete, Japan was becoming part of the world. Within the group they must continue to help one another, adapting to and learning all they could of their husband's country. The old timers must help the new. Their comfort, knowledge and sense of humour would reduce the phenomena of culture shock. She sat down and everyone clapped.

Later, against a yawning, sun-filled window Janet Okuda poured tea from a large chrome pot. The women queued in an orderly line, beneath conversation cups clattered delicately. Janet Okuda lowered her head, smiled wetly at Natsuko and tweaked her chin. With a spatula knife she presented a slice of crumbly cake, sprinkled with sesame seeds. Frances and Natsuko walked back to the groups of chatting women. From a distance heads moved gently, like heavy flowers on long stems. They steered into them and settled. But, although they were greeted and talked to, Natsuko saw her mother did not melt among the teacups and words, as did the other women. She sat tense and straight, teacup knocking thinly on the saucer, her expression expectant and wooden, thoughts folded inside her. Slowly the other women released her, carefully, so that she would not feel it, and projected their concern the other way. Frances was left alone.

But soon Janet Okuda came over with a cup of tea. She looked at Natsuko critically.

'She's growing so pretty, Frances. Her eyes are so round, and her hair almost as blonde as yours. That's unusual. Really, you would hardly know there was a Japanese half to her, she looks so like you. If I had ever had children, I should have wished them to look like Natsuko.' Her eyes speared into Natsuko, she spoke loudly and everyone turned their heads. Frances seemed pleased and ruffled her daughter's hair. But Natsuko bit sesame seeds between her front teeth, filled with sudden shame, sure of an unpleasant depth to Janet Okuda's words. She noticed now there were a number of bristly grey hairs on her chin, and fine cracks through her lips. Janet Okuda leaned towards them.

'There is something I want to ask you, Frances. You are one of our oldest members. Can you think of anything we can possibly do to help Jean? You know, of course, what's happened?' Janet Okuda showed surprise as Frances shook her head. She leaned nearer, the bulge of her midriff distended under the soft blue fabric of her dress.

'I'm surprised you don't know. But it was only last week. Her husband has gone off with a Japanese woman, someone he picked up in a bar. Sounds terribly cheap and tawdry to me. But he was always one for the bars and the women, we all know that. Being married to Jean never changed him. She has been so wonderful, of course, gone along with him from the beginning. Always said it was the way here and didn't mean much, and that inflation would bring him home quicker than nagging. But look where it has landed her now. Don't know what she'll do. She's still in a state of shock, and hoping it will just blow over.'

Listening, Frances' face grew tight and small. Natsuko saw thin lines beneath her eyes and the dry powderiness of her skin. Frances did not speak.

'Talk to her, Frances. I want her to know we are all here if she needs us. It is most important she should feel our support.' Frances nodded mutely.

53

Later they went for more tea and passed the woman, Jean. Frances hesitated and momentarily stopped, but somebody already stood talking to her. She gave a small, bleak shrug and her words came clearly to Natsuko and Frances.

'They revert. As soon as they get back here. They seem so different when you meet them abroad. But society here is so rigid, like one of their stiff flower arrangements, all spontaneity sacrificed to form. They have to revert. They can't live back here unless they do.' Her voice was bitter splinters, welling up, breaking into her face.

Natsuko looked up then and saw her mother staring at the woman. An angular agony in Frances' face revealed something that had no shape. Then, quickly, she turned and walked on.

But, sitting again on the edge of her chair, the cup perched on her knee, Frances' eyes still flitted nervously over the woman. Natsuko watched in apprehension. Although she understood nothing she felt her mother marooned upon a fragment of feeling, rushing further and further from solid shore. But the nuances she caught in Frances refused identity. They passed sometimes in a shadow across her face, hovering behind her eyes or on the edge of spoken words. Slowly, this anxiety penetrated Natsuko, gathering in her, pulpy with her mother's fear.

Now, further up the hospital corridor a short, stout nun came out of a door and walked on towards the next. She was the one who had first shown Natsuko to her mother when she was born. In the middle of the corridor she stopped, bending awkwardly to tie a shoelace. Beneath her habit the backs of round calves appeared, and the end of short stockings about her knees. Over the elastic the flesh of her thighs spilt in soft folds. Straightening, she walked on, nodding as she passed

54

Kazuo and the other nun. Natsuko saw her father smile briefly. Then, in his face, the eyebrows drew tightly together again, between them deep creases flared up into his forehead.

Inside Natsuko felt herself gathered to a small tight ball. Beyond the corridor the future pushed out, the dark shaft of a well, whose end she could not see. Behind her she felt sure Hiroko smiled quietly.

[5]

Not knowing what to do with them, realizing they should not always be left with the maid, Hiroko, he called them into the study with him. Placing his hands on the desk, pushing back the chair resignedly, he looked at them sitting upon the couch. Since Frances left for England he felt the weight of the children, they disturbed his work. Tidying the papers on the desk he placed reference books on Japanese sword fittings to the left, the sheets of the unfinished article on top, weighed down by a stone seal in the shape of a lion. On the paper ink had dried, thick and glossy. Verticle strips of cross-hatched characters stood out strongly from the page. April sun illuminated the manuscript, cutting through the loquat tree outside the window. He swivelled round in his chair to the blue glazed pot of the *hibachi* brazier beside him. Pressing his knees against it he picked the metal chopsticks out of powdered grey ashes, and turned the glowing charcoal at the centre. Raw warmth fanned up at him, he held his fingers to it.

'You may draw the armour today.' He looked proudly at the two fine suits sitting side by side in front of a screen. Had he been offered a similar chance, as a child, he would have felt honoured. Then these same suits of armour were locked away, in a stone storehouse in the garden of the family home. Their black lacquer boxes resembled house shrines and, like esoteric Bhuddist images, were opened only once a year, not for viewing, but for cleaning. Then, had his father allowed

56

him this privilege, to touch, look and draw the mass of intricate metal plates and lacing that made up the armour, he would have been overwhelmed.

For his childhood had held little light relief. It was study, lessons, and again more study punctuated by exams. Pressure was built up for months before these exams, especially the ones for middle school. That day had been like a white hot poker in his mind. His whole academic future, and the course of his life until the day he died, depended upon the passing of exams, and entry to the right academic spheres. Each examination was a stage, each took him deeper into life, nearer adulthood, further from the permissive pre-school years. Looking back he remembered those years as the sun reflected in rockpools, as he caught tiny, burrowing sand-crabs on a beach in Shimoda. Or again he found them in the smells of disturbed grass, as he rushed through it one day, waving a butterfly net. He could still see the butterfly, yellow and huge, flitting before him against the sun. His eyes had watered with the effort of holding it pinned there.

Then he reached kindergarten age and the family had ceremoniously presented him with his first desk and a stout leather satchel. He was measured for a uniform of thick black serge. From then on the brightest orb in his life was the electric light on his desk. Play became filled with guilt, and the warning expressions of adults against such irresponsibility. Like ripples on the surface of a pond, the lifelong obligatory duties and debts of *giri* and *on* spread out from his small body, clearer, denser, further reaching with each year of life. The very state of living, he was taught, was a debt. Virtue could only be found in dedicating himself actively to the job of gratitude, to the repayment of each part of the debt. The layers of obligation started from the highest pinnacle, of

Emperor and country, and spread out in a triangle through duties to parents, ancestors, teachers and work, down to the very basic duty to his own name. This must always be clear, admitting neither failure nor ignorance, fulfilling each Japanese propriety, observing respectful behaviour, never living beyond means, curbing all inappropriate displays of emotion, reputing all insult with honourable vendetta.

They were the descendants of a *samurai* family, and that pride and dignity embued each action of Kazuo's father. He instilled its traditions into his sons. A man must rise above danger, and bear pain without flinching. But the vendetta of the sword was only one of the virtues that may be needed upon occasion. Stoicism and self-control were equally required by self-respect. Once, soon after he started kindergarten, his father had caught Kazuo playing with matches. Solemnly he had taken the box from him and struck a match. Taking Kazuo's finger he pushed it into the flame, and briefly held it there. The pain had been intense, he remembered it still, but more than that he felt his father's eyes, boring deeper within him than any flame could reach.

His father had also many famous tales of *samurai* stoicism. He remembered one well, told him soon after the match incident, about Count Katsuu, who died in 1899. When he was a boy his testicles had been torn by a dog. While a doctor operated on him, his father held a sword to his nose. 'If you utter one cry,' he told him, 'you will die in a way that at least will not be shameful.' This story had haunted Kazuo for months. He dreamed frequently of it in lurid detail, waking in the night, covered in sweat, biting his lips to make no sound, praying his father would never know his cowardice in facing this exemplary story.

The noise of Natsuko's feet, kicking the base of the couch,

pulled him back from his thoughts. He cleared his throat and Riichi looked up, obedient. Natsuko just flopped back in the couch, lips pushed out in silent pout.

He looked at them, and knew despair. Against his better judgement their upbringing was so different from his own. He begrudged them nothing of their mother's culture, but there seemed no meeting point with his own. They were the products of the local American school, as Frances insisted. He looked at them, slouched and undisciplined, Western now in the worst sense, in spite of their Japanese blood. He loved them, but he had not foreseen this for his children when he married. Anger with Frances overwhelmed him. Could she not see clearly their children's future? What hope had they here, growing up in this irresponsible way, of finding their right place? They appeared to him inwardly soft, and outwardly slovenly. He wanted then fiercely to break through the ignorant net Frances had thrown about the children. He wanted them at least to understand that part of him within themselves. He wished them in every true sense to have a choice. Frances saw strength only in rebelling against convention, seizing happiness in spite of obstacles, emphasizing wherever she could the lonely stand of the individual. For Kazuo all strength was in conforming, in being part of the whole plan, in fulfilling to his best each obligation as he saw it. He could do no more than sympathize with Frances' wish always to fight, to stand alone in the solitary confinement of some crochety, irrelevant and totally useless point of view. He wished his children to know there was another way.

He was conscious of never learning to talk to them on their level. It was easier always to instruct, as he did the classes at the University, where his lectures on Japanese history were listened to with interest and respect for his learning. Opening the drawer of the desk he took from it paper and pencils. There was peace without Frances. He was unused yet to the novelty, and the thought was always with him. He wished she would never come back.

Riichi drew quickly. Kazuo Akazawa was pleased at his interest. Perhaps, he thought, the boy felt the beauty of these tiny facets of metal, laced with braid and leather into wonderfully pliable armour. Or maybe the proud ridged bowls of the helmets, with their winged horns and tasselled bows, impressed him. He was hatching in small neat squares of plate firmly, as if each mattered to the whole design. His eyes moved from paper to armour and back again, bright and keen.

Watching him Kazuo remembered the sword incident, and before that Riichi's strong wish to learn *kendo*. In spite of Frances' heated disapproval he clung on until she gave way. Kazuo wondered then if it was really too late? If he was to bring the two children in here each day, like this, and enlighten them in a consistent manner upon different aspects of their heritage. He had done little, in spite of all his own learning. Whatever had rubbed off on his children was but a particle of all he could teach them. Until now Frances had her way. And shutting the door of his study he lost himself in history and art, and felt replenished. So that, when he emerged, he could conduct himself in dignified resignation. Carefully, he had constructed a shell about himself. Now, in Frances' absence, he felt like something frozen put out in the sun. For the first time he saw he had given his children nothing of himself. Now, while Frances was away, he would begin to rectify this. So he stood behind Riichi and began to explain.

'The lacing is in the *shikimi* style, Riichi. Before that they laced in another way, the *kibiki*, but that had two disadvantages. It needed a great many holes to accommodate it, and much more braid. When wet it all became a terrible weight.'

Natsuko was not drawing. From the corner of his eye he saw her blank page. Although only ten, he found her more difficult to reach than Riichi. She slid her eyes up sideways at him, in the same resentful manner as her mother. He must always wonder what he had done wrong, although he had yet to address her directly.

'You don't want to draw the armour, Natsuko?'

'No.'

He sighed. 'Go and look out of the window. Perhaps there you will find something.' He hoped she would not notice his defeat.

She went. He watched her stand, belly pushed out to take her weight against the window, back arched, one foot crossed behind the other. Her casualness made him feel superfluous. She appeared compact and distant. It was easier with Riichi, he was seventeen, nearly an adult, and they had their sex in common. There were interests they might soon share, and in character he was pliant. Something in Natsuko could not be so led. He left her alone and returned to Riichi.

All Natsuko could think was, she is gone. Gone. She will not come back. It is nearly as if she is dead. She could not believe the promise to return, in spite of her mother holding her close and saying, 'It will not be for long. You know I couldn't possibly leave you all for too long. It will be just a few weeks. I expect I shall be back before you know I have gone.'

Crushed into her mother's body, Natsuko sensed a strange, tight desperation from her. And in her mind she saw again

61

now, far away on the tarmac, the door of the plane, shutting. The windows were tiny, giving nothing. She searched each disc separately for her mother's face. But all she found was her own panic, hurting inside until it burst in her veins, flowing out in tears she could not stop. She had not once asked a question, afraid to hear the answers. But a few nights before her father sat on the edge of her bed, unasked, and talked mysteriously of what was wrong with her mother, and when she might return from England. It was all she did not want to hear, and confused her further. She wished to be left a blank pain. It was worse now, with a few obscure details wedged in the hurt. Looking up at him from the pillow she had concentrated on his shadow, thrown by the bedside lamp on to the wall, and the silhouette of his lips as he talked. Inside her something turned off. She knew she must wait, quite still, until the voice finished, before she could breathe again. She held herself clenched, trying to fortify her thin defence. But the words wheedled and squirmed through to the soft, defenceless core of her. She felt their settling in cold hard drops. She heard him say her mother was very ill. Yet the illness was not one seen in an X-ray or a blood test. Nor could a knife cut it out, or medicine repair it. She must heal on her own, from the inside out. And that might take a long time. There was yet no way to say how long. The words gave neither hope nor end. On the wall his lips moved rhythmically, a splinter of short hairs fanned up on the crown of his head.

'Don't you want to hear? Are you not interested, Natsuko? Can't you even look at me while I talk?' His voice cut into her suddenly, harshly. She turned, looking up at him then. But he was already standing up. Abruptly he switched off the light and walked from the room, saying only a sharp goodnight at the door.

She breathed. But the deadness inside her did not lift. Her father's anger stirred no feeling. She was only relieved he was gone, and turned to the blackness of the wall again. But after a while the words had begun to move about, shifting around in her, burrowing deeper and deeper until there was not a part of her left, without holes of pain and fear.

Now tears blurred her eyes and the study window before her. She hated this room, and wished their father would not call them to it. Lying at the back of the house, down a passage, it was dark. Except for one side, where she now stood, trees shrouded the windows, crowding against them. Leaves appeared sometimes ragged, sometimes fleshy, dusty in Summer, oily in rain, thick and black with evening light. In a breeze, claws of holly scratched against the glass. Even in Summer it was cool here, in an unnatural way.

She stared at the lawn, sloping down to cryptomeria and Japanese yew trees. The grass was still yellowed and dead after the Winter, but in patches green bristles pushed through. In a sheltered spot the first buds of the cherry tree had already opened. Nearby fallen petals of magnolia lay strewn about, a rotted soggy brown, like pieces of wet toast. Riichi's pencil scratched clearly in the silence behind her. Its concentration made Natsuko angry. She wanted to turn and stare at him. But then she would see the armour. Already the black slits of its mouth and eyes stroked her back, as they sat, side by side, in front of a low calligraphy screen. After the grandparents died and their house was sold, the armour came to them from the storehouse. She remembered the tight little building, tall as the house, with a metal door and walls two feet thick, windowless and sombre, filled with family treasure and junk. Now, free of their black lacquer boxes, supported on wooden frames the armour lived in the study, admired by many. From stocky waists and breast plates grew the flaps of skirts and shoulders. Hanging from these were midget legs and long loose arms with iron fingers. One was blue laced with a brocaded dragon covering the cuirass, and a helmet of curled ear flaps. The other, threaded with red, had been sometime attacked by moths, fearless of the head sunken deep among enormous shoulders, or the flat horns soaring off the helmet. Side by side they sat together like sentinels, their presence chilling the room, projecting more than human disdain. It might have all been bearable, but for the face masks of polished black iron, fierce enough to frighten bad spirits and enemies, their ferocity was whiskered and bearded. The red laced one had a stiff blond moustache, the blue one a soft white beard, spread sparsely over his chin, startling against the dark iron face. Beneath, their mouths grimaced wildly, filled with iron teeth. Above the snarling noses their eyes were empty holes. Sometimes the faces screamed fiendishly at Natsuko, sometimes they mocked with hideous laughter. But always, each night, they stretched up to her room above the study. Reaching out from beneath her bed they mesmerized the dark. Sometimes, even in daylight, their faces slipped between her thoughts. Then the air around her corroded, and the house seemed diseased by the silence of their empty eyes.

Just thinking now, knowing they were behind her, watching, waiting, made the walls grow tight about Natsuko, until they pressed in from all sides. In spite of her father and Riichi, sitting behind, unaware, neutralizing the room, she had to get out. Abruptly she turned and ran, without a word of explanation.

She came to the kitchen, knowing there would be Hiroko, and some activity. Anything to lift the feeling of the study.

And Hiroko was there, preparing the lunch, lifting a small red octopus in a wire net strainer from a pot on the stove. Steam rose off the boiling water and the short, thick tentacles. Pink suckers puckered each leg like buttons. Hiroko took a knife to the chopping board as Natsuko watched, and sliced off the limbs. Inside the flesh was white and smooth. But Natsuko thought of the suckers, the waving legs, and knew she would not eat it. Her mother never cooked such things. From the boiling water steam frosted the window above the sink, and coated the air with a hot, rough smell. Each time Hiroko pressed down with the knife a muscle pulled at the side of her mouth.

'He must long for his own kind of food,' Hiroko had said, the first day after Frances left, stirring bean paste soup, washing under the tap a pale clump of long-stemmed mushrooms, with tiny pinhead caps. At the table Natsuko had eaten grilled eel and papery strips of black seaweed resentfully. Now, watching Hiroko at the chopping board, slicing tentacles neatly, Natsuko was filled with jubilation. It is only, she thought, that she cannot make thin flaky pastry, or gravies of wine and cream.

Seeing Natsuko in the doorway, annoyance spread in Hiroko's face.

'Always watching. Have you nothing better to do? Go and call them to eat, it's just about ready.'

Natsuko walked back through the dining-room, on her way to the study. Since her mother left the table was set differently. It was laid with blue and white china rice and tea bowls, small rectangular plates and lacquer chopsticks. They ate Japanese food now every day, at Kazuo's request and with Hiroko's compliance. And Kazuo had decided, throwing himself into the role of organizer, that they should all eat together, Hiroko was part of the family. Her place at the table was between himself and Riichi.

They came at once from the study, hungry, settling on their chairs with robust anticipation. Natsuko was alone with her feelings now her mother was gone. Kazuo and Riichi ate with relish, like deserters from a battle. Natsuko was left to watch the moving bulges in the side of their cheeks, and their amiable exchanges.

Between them Hiroko was busy. From a large electric rice cooker on the table she doled out the rice with a flat wooden spoon, scraping it against the side of each bowl, clearing it of sticky grains. In glutinous lumps the rice steamed, moist and hot. She poured tea for them all, refilling the small bowls as soon as they were empty. Inclining her head coquettishly, she asked if Kazuo and Riichi wanted more, in unnecessary politeness. They affirmed with a grunt, the raised bowls of rice half covering their faces, chopsticks shovelling into their mouths.

Natsuko looked at the uneaten slices of tentacle on her plate, the pale smooth suckers rimmed by a thin black edge. In the bowl each grain of rice was covered with a hot starchy glaze. She left the octopus, but picked up the bowl of rice and began to eat, listening to the intimate, wheedling tone Hiroko insinuated into each pretentious form of verb; a less complicated language would have been equally polite. Every so often she pulled out a giggly little laugh, sometimes shielding it with her hand. She enjoyed these meals. It was only when she looked at Natsuko, sour and broody across the table, food untouched before her, that her eyes resettled for a moment in their usual inscrutability.

Now she was pouring tea with care, one hand holding the wicker handle of the pot, a finger of the other hand resting on the lid. She lowered her eyes assuming demureness. Her hair was pinned severely back, but a few strands escaped, fanning out upon her forehead.

Holding the tea bowl cupped in his hands, Kazuo Akazawa noticed again the thick lid, and the narrow lobe of ear, blending smoothly into the cheek. Upon the teapot lid the finger was small as a child's, the nail an oval shell. Straightening then she glanced up at him, and did not hurry to avert her eyes when she saw him looking at her.

Watching them Natsuko saw the moment, wrenched away from the ticking clock, stilled and held between them, like a bubble. Hanging in the air, surrounded by air, filled with air, yet separate, special, closed and still. She knew something she could give no name to had passed between them, something ignited, fluid and warm. She saw it established, and what could not be expressed burnt within her. She felt sweat on the palms of her hands, and beating blood in her head. She knew she must break the bubble, so that the moments could flow again.

Quickly then, she thrust out her hands, pushing everything before her. The rice bowls and hot tea tipped over, streaming across the table top, trickling to her knees. The warmth penetrating quickly through her jeans. Standing up abruptly, she pushed back forcefully with her leg at the chair. It fell over behind her with a blunt thud.

'It's horrible. I hate it. I don't want any more of this awful food. She can't cook. She can't do anything.' She screamed it out and ran.

Half turning at the door she saw them, sitting in amazement. Riichi with the bowl of rice half-way to his mouth, her father's face clouded by anger. But on Hiroko she saw only the eyes, bright as jet, hard and hating.

He told them at breakfast the next morning. He had thought it out well. First he had said to himself, she is to be punished, she must be taught some discipline and her place. But then he came back to the beginning. It was Frances. She encouraged spontaneity that now, in the present stress, over-reached itself. The child knew no other way to show she missed her mother. Because she was difficult, because he did not know how to approach her, he must try harder. The idea came to him then, he was pleased. And he himself badly needed the break.

At first she seemed happy, her face lit up.

'It is so near,' he told her. 'And the valley is sheltered. The cherry trees are already in bloom there.'

The brightness flickered in her face. 'Will she come too? Hiroko?'

She looked at the half open kitchen door. Inside, over a running tap, was the sound of plates, slithering together into a bowl of soapy water.

'Of course.' It had not occurred to him to think she would not. He did not feel he could manage Natsuko entirely on his own. Animation fell from her. She slumped back in the chair, lower lip pushed out in an ugly pout.

No, he thought. She must learn. Some things she must accept.

They took the road through the mountain tunnel, near the house. It ran for five kilometres, sooty and dank, like the tunnel of an earthworm. Cars came at them from the opposite direction flashing their headlights. Natsuko thought of the great mound of earth rising over them, hundreds of feet. She thought of the weight pressing down on the tunnel, and wished it soon would end.

At last they sped out. The sudden glare of white and green, the airy bowl of sky, took her breath away. The road wound down between tall slopes of conifer trees. Bamboo grass reached to the kerb, there was a sweet smell in the air.

Riichi sat in front with Kazuo. The back seat held Hiroko and Natsuko, who pushed herself tight against the corner, keeping her face to the window. Hiroko had refused to speak to her since yesterday. Natsuko was glad. Now it was established they hated each other. There was no longer a necessity to obey any rules.

'We'll go first to the fishing ponds,' said Kazuo, from the front seat.

For already they were there, in the small airless valley of Arima Spa. They stopped at a traffic light. Outside Natsuko's window a street pushed up to the high *torii* arch of a Shinto shrine. Stalls covered by red and white bunting lined the road selling edibles and trinkets. There were always stalls out on feast days and festivals. Near the traffic light was a barrow of cooked snails, their large shells crowded on to a charcoal grill. A man stood, snail in hand, pulling the soft body from the shell with a tooth pick, bending his head low to bite off a piece. A sharp briney smell came in the car window. At the top of the street, through the shrine archway, was the pale frost of cherry trees in bloom. Then Kazuo turned the car sharply away, up a craggy road between old inns, souvenir shops and modern hotels. Twice they passed the steamy plume of a hot water geyser escaping from a pipe. There were many geysers in Arima, tamed into the baths of inns and hotels. The road became narrower, stopping suddenly at a footbridge. Here they parked the car. After the drone of the engine, it was silent and warm. Almost from their feet steep wooded hills soared up. Above the sky was far away. Natsuko felt at the bottom of a cup. From the footbridge she looked at the shallow moving water, listening to it rushing between foliage and stones. In the trees around was the sound of birds. She looked up into the thick branches above, layer upon layer, receding upwards, dense and peaceful, and drew a deep breath. For a moment these things took the edge off Hiroko's presence.

But then, beyond the footbridge, through the netted wire, she saw the movement of people and colour. From a bright blue booth Kazuo bought tickets, and counted them in through the gate. Immediately it was another world, netted off in the fold of the hills. Crowds in holiday mood and matching clothes, swarmed about the three huge fishing tanks, that on split levels backed up into the hillside. Kazuo and Riichi marched ahead over a red zigzag bridge, across the middle pool. Behind them Natsuko stopped and, looking down, saw the dark shadow of the bridge upon the water. In it, like a thick blowing curtain, moved the bodies of a shoal of fish. She stood quite still, watching their smooth undulation. When she reached the end of the bridge the others were already entering the small thatched hut, to hire rods, a bucket and to buy bait.

Inside the hut it was dim, it smelt fishy and the concrete floor was wet. At one side was a bucket of bloody water, a knife lying next to it, and on the ground a silvery smear of scales. Outside the open door a man knelt beside a wooden tray. Natsuko looked over his shoulder and saw the limp, pale bodies of worms, mashed to a pasty bait. With a large pronged fork the man pressed down upon the slimy mess, his body swaying forward. It was this they carried with them in a metal bowl. And with his bare fingers Riichi kneaded it about the hook, eager to start.

Pushing between people Kazuo made room for them all about the fishing pool. There was even a stool for Natsuko to sit on, and a place for the bucket of water at her feet. Standing behind Riichi, clasping their four hands together about the rod, Kazuo helped swing the line, casting it into the middle of the tank. Together they swayed back, swung their arms, and pitched with a loud cry. Beside them Hiroko clapped as the line fell into the water.

On the low stool Natsuko seemed very near the water. Its surface stretched out in a shiny grey sheet. She was aware of a border of faces and laughter. But between that was greyness. Everywhere she looked seemed grey. The pale oily water, the concrete surround of the tank sinking purposefully, a wet grey watermark around the perimeter. She saw the sky had greyed, and the green of the trees was depressed and sombre. And in the water, a deeper grey still, were the sharp desperate movements of fish. Slim mottled fish swarmed near the surface. Above the water baited lines flicked back and forth, beneath the shoal moved with them, oiled and pliant. Occasionally an eager fish jumped clear of the water, beneath the dark shadows of larger ones moved sluggishly about the bottom of the tank.

As Natsuko watched, a fish broke the water again and fell back with a splash. She wanted to shout out to it, angered by its foolishness and ignorance. The grotesque conspiracy above the water, and the fact that they had paid to be part of it filled her with agitation. Jostling about the pool, faces grinned unceasingly beneath holiday hats. In the sun colours grew reckless. A garish checked cap fell into the water and floated away under the red bridge. Two coy lovers offered each other the line. At a bucket a child dipped its hands into a mass of squirming bodies and laughed. And all the while, above the still water, the rods flicked quickly in and out. From their ends silver bodies twisted in the sun. The writhings were small, without consequence, quickly grasped in a hand and ripped from a line.

Suddenly Riichi gave a cry, feeling the tug of his first fish. The line swung out of the water, taut, spiralling wildly in the air. Immediately Kazuo helped him steady the rod, brought in the line and made Riichi take the fish in his hand. Together they tugged at the hook and line in its open mouth. The fish slipped from Riichi's hand and swung across the water. They tried again, pulling harder, and ripped the fish free. Revulsion puckered up tight in Natsuko as they threw it into the bucket at her feet. She pulled back on the stool, feeling the water splash her bare leg, trickling into her sock. She could not look into the bucket. Almost at once Riichi threw in another fish, then a third. She was sure they must be dead, lying limp at the bottom of the bucket. Instead, when she looked, they were swimming feverishly round and round, knocking against each other. The thin line of their backbones curved tightly to the shape of the bucket.

They soon tired of the small silver fish and moved down to the lower tank. Here big grey carp swam, slowly, deeper down. They took much longer to catch, less enthusiastic about their fate. But at last Riichi's line grew taut, the rod curving pliantly to the surface of the water. Suddenly the fish appeared and came, twisting and swinging towards them, on the end of the line. Natsuko ran back a short distance, horrified. The fish landed near her feet, flapping and jumping, soon covered with dust and grit. It was large and strong. She ran back still further, afraid of it touching her. It jumped suddenly and she saw daylight clear beneath it. Behind Riichi, Hiroko squealed. They could not manage it, and called the attendant. Kneeling to the fish, holding it down with one hand, he ripped the hook swiftly from its throat. It came away with a lump of flesh. At that moment the gills dilated widely, showing tunnels of red light through its open mouth. They picked it up by the tail, and flung it in to the bucket. Riichi and Kazuo smiled proudly. Behind them Hiroko clapped.

Natsuko stared at them seeing suddenly only their grinning mouths, devouring their faces, disgorging teeth and imperturbability. She held her breath unable to either scream or weep. They did not see the bucket was small, that the fish convulsed, half in, half out, that the water oozed with blood.

Turning her back she ran, unable to see any more the desperate fish, the grinning crowds with cameras and chewing gum, and the flicking lines across the water.

She ran to the bright, bland shape of the children's playground. There she found a yellow swing, and sat down. Without taking her feet from the ground, she moved it gently to and fro. Its metal joints protested hoarsely. She closed her eyes and after a while it all began to drift away. From the swing she looked again at the wooded slopes, and felt the thick, closed silence. The sharp chirping of birds came to her. Near her foot a black and blue speckled beetle walked awkwardly past, antenna waving before it. A sleek beige lizard ran over a stone and under a bush. From a large wooden building behind the playground came the smell of frying fish. She closed her eyes and listened to the birds.

The sun on her face made her skin heavy. It seemed a long while since she ran into the playground. She knew soon they must come for her. Now and then, through half-closed eyes, she squinted against the sun, keeping track of them. They had moved from the tank, over to the counter for weighing the

73

fish. She saw her father pay and hand the bucket to the attendant. Then they turned, coming towards her.

Kazuo pushed the yellow swing, the ground jerked suddenly away from her. His hand grasped the thick rope near her face, a fishy odour stirred her nose. Turning she saw the wet gleam to his knuckles. They stood round the swing smiling, asking if she was enjoying herself. The fish would be fried for them in the restaurant. This would be their lunch, they told her.

Inside the restaurant it was crowded, filled with tight, pungent smells. All the metal tables and chairs were full in the first room, so they left their shoes and stepped up into the *tatami* matted room at the back. Here they found a low table near a window overlooking the playground, and sat upon white cushions on the floor around it.

Beneath the fried fish the room smelt strongly of rush mats, septic tanks and beer. Around them people were noisy, babies cried. At the next table a group of labourers lounged upon the matting, picking their teeth, skin leathered red, mouths filled by gold crowns.

Kazuo ordered beer and had a glass placed by Hiroko too. When it came she poured it for him, kneeling up to the table on her cushion. The brown bottle was frosted and wet with condensation, dark against the thin pink material of her new Spring dress. She poured, careful that the beer would not overflow the glass. It fizzed up, frothy and white above the rim, then sank back. Kazuo drank it down in long gulps. Hiroko refilled his glass and then sipped daintily from her own. Natsuko saw it gradually relax them. Her father's nose and cheeks turned pink. Hiroko giggled behind her hand. Soon they ordered more.

For lunch the small fish came first, crisp and shrunken. On

blue and white rectangular plates they lay like charred sticks, fins a papery yellow, heads shrivelled. They placed one before Natsuko. A cluster of blue chrysanthemums were painted across the corner of the plate. But she looked and could not eat, remembering the spiralling line in the water, the writhing silver end.

At first they were too busy to notice her. Holding the fish just below the head with chopsticks, they lowered their mouths. Across the table Natsuko saw again the pink curling tip of Hiroko's tongue. The head of the fish disappeared into her mouth, her teeth snapped shut upon it. Then the body of the fish was pulled away, its trunk splintering into white-edged flakes. Around the table their jaws moved rhythmically. Within them Natsuko imagined the fish, fried eyes, gills and bones pounded to wet pulp. She pushed her cushion back against the wall, and knew they would tell her to eat.

Dumbly, shaking her head, she refused. The more they persuaded the more vividly she felt the head in her mouth, her tongue brushing the dry wrinkled surface, the cooked lips and fins.

'No,' she said again.

'Natsuko. I said eat it. Natsuko,' Kazuo shouted, losing patience.

'The eyes are still in.' She knew she should not have told them. For immediately they laughed.

'They're crisp, Natsuko. Like peanuts,' Riichi teased.

But Kazuo was annoyed now. There seemed no way to please the child. She had learnt it all from her mother. Stretching across the table he lifted the fish with his chopsticks brusquely, from her plate to his. There was a looseness in him after the beer, making it difficult to control his resentment. Fishing with Riichi had produced a companionship between them he had not felt before. He knew now, undisturbed by Frances, it was possible to salvage something of the relationship between himself and his son. The thought made him feel good, almost lightheaded. It made him drink far too much beer. So that, although he tried to contain it, the woman Hiroko filled him again. He could not forget her presence, her watchfulness of him. He was aware of her all the time now, since Frances left. She was like a line drawn taut in his head. As he awoke in the mornings she came into his mind, and stayed through the day. He tried to push the thought of her away, but she grew in him like a disease, until he was filled by an aching impatience.

Something snapped in him then, and anger rose up for the stubborn child across the table. Her eyes flicked over him always. It was as if Frances sat there, watching, checking. He clenched the muscles of his jaw, turning his face away.

He was angry, she knew, but she feared much more the expression in Hiroko's eyes. Hand spread across mouth, thumb resting lightly on her cheekbone, she giggled. But above the hand her eyes were mocking and victorious. Natsuko looked down at the tight woven floor and knew it was the greatest mistake, to admit she could not eat the eyes. Now she was vulnerable to Hiroko.

There was neither tail nor head to the carp. It came cut into pieces. From the fleshy lump she pulled off a few white flakes, and ate without tasting, the aubergine pickles and the rice.

[6]

Directly inside the door of the inn a little bridge of polished wood arched over an artificial stream. Plants and a pale metal stork were arranged on white gravel at one side. This deposited them before the high step up on to the inn. Natsuko was delighted with the bridge and stream, but they stayed only long enough to leave their baggage. Then Kazuo led them across the road to the shrine they had seen from the traffic light.

Cherry blossom overpowered the small courtyard, people massed beneath it. It was one of the traditional weekends for blossom viewing. Natsuko recognized some of the faces from the fishing tanks. She looked up at the blossom-filled branches, at paper lanterns and swaying windbells. In front of her Kazuo was telling Riichi of famous blossom viewing parties of the past, commemorated on equally famous screens and scrolls. He overflowed with details about their sophistication and elegance, the special costumes of the court, the food eaten, the poems composed. Natsuko listened while observing the litter-strewn ground about her, unable to see in the mess any connection with the esoteric past. Mixed with fallen petals were soft drink cans, disposable lunch boxes, half eaten buns. A plane droned low overhead, nearing Osaka airport. She kicked a rotten apple core away from her feet. Behind her a transistor radio blared popular music. People sat beneath trees, with their lunch boxes and flasks of green tea. Against a wall a group of farmers sat drinking from cans of *sake* and beer. From their radio came the pulse of folk music, over-powering the rock band on the one behind. As they neared the farmers, one of the men stood up, quite drunk, and began to dance, clapping his hands, his face red above his swaying body. Nearby on a bench sat four bent old women, with thin tight buns and toothless gums. Their faces, impassive above drab coloured *kimono*, broke into smiles at the dancing man. From another group a solid matron in sober *kimono* stood up, tying a narrow scarf about her hair. She hitched her *kimono* above pink underskirts into her *obi* sash, and joined the farmer to dance to the radio. Around them everyone clapped and sang out the chorus. Soon they were joined by another woman, with under *kimono* of almond green.

Natsuko hung back, liking the dancing women and the folk music. Through its cracks she could see the screens and poems her father described. But the raucous farmers with their reddened faces, the close jostle of people and tired children, the litter of cans and cellophane bags overwhelmed it all and made her fretful. She was glad when her father turned suddenly, pointing to the path. A narrow line of red arches twisted up into the steep wooded hill behind the shrine, to a pilgrimage point. Above it was the pink of another glade of cherry trees.

Kazuo led the way. Narrow and rough, the path went upwards steeply. At intervals they passed under the low, red lacquered *torii* arches. They were old and weathered, the lacquer cracked and splintered, the inscriptions written on them faint. Deep ruts in the path acted as steps. Breathing hard Natsuko pulled herself up, clinging to branches and woody shrubs. Soon a thick roof of trees was above them, it was dim and close. In places the path was covered thickly by fallen pine needles and rotted cones. Above, among the dark matted branches of firs and evergreens was the bright sap green of new leaves. The air smelt strong, sweet with damp soil and pines.

Already they were up quite high, and still climbing swiftly. Natsuko's legs ached with the effort. Above the path went on as far as she could see, almost vertical above their heads. The others were some distance in front. Ahead was the bent swell of Hiroko's hips, the strong muscles of her legs hard and tight as she climbed. Natsuko hurried to catch up. The path, level for some yards, twisted up again. She held on to a thick tuft of dry grass, pulling up on it. Suddenly it gave way in her hand, a clump of soft soil spilling over her leg. She stumbled backwards, her foot twisting over, pain wrapping about her ankle. It eased as she steadied herself and straightened, but climbing was slower, and uncomfortable. She called up to them.

'Well, come a bit further. There's a clearing here. You can wait for us and rest,' said Kazuo, coming back, taking her hand and helping her up.

'We'll go on. Hiroko can stay with you here.' Kazuo turned, Riichi following. They began to climb again. Soon they were absorbed by foliage.

They were just at the edge of the cherry glade she had seen from below. Woven among the other trees blossom spread upwards in patches. The floor of the clearing was dry and earthy, grassy weeds fringed the sides. She walked to the edge and looked down the wooded drop to the temple below. They were a long way above it. The cherry trees filled the court-yard, obscuring the heads below, the blossom reminding her of candy floss. For a moment the farmer's radio was silent, and the jingle of windbells drifted up. Then the radio started again, fainter. She turned back into the clearing. A few large

79

stones edged one side of it. Hiroko sat on one, fanning herself with a handkerchief.

It was quiet. The noise from the shrine was far away, hardly touching the peace. In the trees was only the sound of small birds. The sunlight pushed between leaves, splattering yellow lozenges on the floor of the clearing. An opening among the treetops showed a patch of sky. A crow flew over. It cawed once, wings flapping lazily against the cloud. Hiroko stood up and wandered off without a word. Natsuko was relieved. Dropping her head back she stretched until the skin of her chin pulled tautly at her neck, and took deep breaths. The sweetness of damp soil and rotted leaves filled her nostrils, the astringency of pine was fresh in her head, the sun warm on her face. She was glad they had come up here, glad she was forced to sit, like this.

'Natsuko.' Hiroko called from the far end of the clearing, smiling, beckoning. Immediately suspicion needled in her but, against the tall trees, Hiroko looked unassuming.

'Come. Look what's here.' She turned, stepping into the long grass at the edge of the clearing, among the trees.

It lay deep among the fallen leaves and grasses, curled up as if it were asleep. And at first she thought it was just sleeping, and dropped on a knee, crouching to the cat. It was white and lay on its side, back curved, paws drawn up together in front. Against the white fur its pads were pink as her palms. The eyes were closed, but the ears stood up in stiff points, alert, etched with a tracery of fine red lines. She touched it with one finger, hesitantly. The fur was soft, but underneath she felt the hardness of it. It did not move. Knowing then it was dead she pulled sharply back, shivering. Above Hiroko watched, as Natsuko stood up she placed a hand on her arm.

'Look,' Hiroko said, bending forward, holding a short stick.

Pushing it under the animal, she turned the cat over. It fell with a small thud, and a cracking of dry leaves.

Natsuko looked only once, quickly before she ran. But the picture of it was there, stamped in her mind now. She knew it would never leave her. The raw pulpy mess of it, skin torn away, the inside alive with swarming black insects, would be with her always. Her stomach heaved and she retched, bending over, holding on to the trunk of a tree. Swallowing hard she forced herself to walk, calmly, back to the row of stones. To appear as unaffected as possible was the only defence against Hiroko.

But under her now the stone was cold. She could not locate the flat, comfortable angle she sat upon before. Looking up through the branches to the sky, she could no longer find beauty. She felt imprisoned, locked in by thick trunks and leafy hands. Now she sensed a secrecy in the woods. Listening, she became aware of constant stirrings, the noises not only of birds, but of insects and small animals. Their movement awoke leaves, breaking twigs, a slithering through grass. She was an intruder, not meant to know the secrets held here, of death and violence. It was all around her, she knew it now. She saw it, alive, in the dense tangle of shrubs and branches, in the gnarled snaking roots of trees. It was another world, full of eyes. They watched her from the thick matted branches. She now saw the weak spearings of sun could never open the clearing with warmth or light. It was cold and savage by day, at night filled by wandering spirits from the temple below.

Faintly, a few bars of radio music drifted up. They must still be dancing, all the old men and women. From where she sat she could just see a corner of temple blossom. It looked overblown and irrelevant now. Instead at the side of the

81

clearing she noticed a tree, splintered, struck by lightning long before. Its dead shaft soared up, bony and white. Near the root the trunk was rotted and mealy.

Hiroko walked back into the clearing. Satisfaction diffused her face. She sat down again on the stone beside Natsuko. Her stockings were laddered, bits of dry stalk and leaf stuck to them. Bending she began to pick them clean. 'Wasn't it horrible?'

Natsuko said nothing, knowing she waited, watching.

'It's been tortured,' Hiroko told her.

'No. No.' She could not hold it back. Horror fell out of her. The end of her voice was a sob.

'Of course. Didn't you see the wire about its neck?'

Once, near the house, she had seen some boys with a puppy. They stood in a circle about it. The puppy was no bigger than their feet, fluffy brown with bright eyes and nose. Each time it rushed to escape it was kicked and stoned. Quickly, she ran away, but the sound of its yelps stayed with her. It was a long time before she could pass the place without looking apprehensively about, feeling she would see its body, lying somewhere, dead and maimed.

'Why? Why did you have to show it to me?' She was afraid she might begin to cry. Her throat was tight, coming out the words hurt.

'You're a big girl now. You should see all things in the world. Everything has its place. Your mother has spoilt you. She has made you soft.'

'No. No.'

'Of course she has.'

'Don't say things like that.'

'But it's true. She has made a baby of you. What will you do in life, if now you can't even look at a dead cat?'

82

'It was more than dead. It was horrible.' Natsuko felt the injustices burning in her.

'It's still dead. Dead things can't hurt you. And stop crying like that.' Hiroko shrugged.

Natsuko wiped her eyes on the back of her hand, Hiroko gave a short taunting giggle.

'You're an *ai no ko*, a half-caste child. You have no place here. I expect you could go to America. They seem to accept everything and everyone in America. Or maybe they would have you in England, or anywhere else in the rest of the world. But it's different here in Japan. You are a dirty stain. There is no place here for you. You will probably have to go away.'

'Stop it. I hate you.' Natsuko sobbed, wetness dribbling down her neck inside her collar.

'It's the truth. But if you don't like it, you had better make up your mind to change. Your mother won't come back. Forget all the things she taught you. It makes you a nuisance to your father. Your brother is different. He tries. Your father is pleased with him.'

From above came the noise of feet and voices. Kazuo and Riichi came into view.

'Don't tell about the cat. Understand?' Hiroko threatened.

Quickly Natsuko wiped her wet cheeks on the hem of her skirt. Hiroko walked to a tree, turned and leaned against it. Rubbing the thick cotton skirt across her eyes, Natsuko heard her laugh again.

She did not know how she had failed to foresee it. She was to share a room with Hiroko. Kazuo and Riichi would have another. The thought was heavy in her stomach. Clutching a small plastic bowl and a cake of soap, she followed Hiroko on the way to the big communal bath. They were identically dressed in blue and white cotton *kimono*, provided by the hotel. Only their narrow sashes were different colours. Natsuko was cold and naked beneath the thin cotton. Winter was officially ended long before, and the hotel was unheated. In the rooms were glazed china *hibachi* braziers, to warm their hands. But the corridors were long draughty avenues of polished wood. Hiroko's bare heels slapped the soles of her slippers, walking ahead.

Steamy air swirled behind the frosted glass door of the women's entrance. Immediately they went inside, it soaked into the *kimono*, which grew suddenly warm and limp about Natsuko. Hiroko took a large orange plastic basket from a pile in the corner, and walked to the shelves at the side of the room.

Turning Natsuko around by the shoulders, she began to untie the sash of her *kimono*. Winding it into a neat ball around her fingers she dropped it into the basket, and pulled the garment from Natsuko's body.

Slatted wooden boards covered the floor, swollen and wet. Curling her toes around a thin plank Natsuko felt diminished by nakedness, and frail. She stared down at her clenched toes and soggy splinters in the wood. Beside her Hiroko undressed.

'Come.' Hiroko turned, leading the way. Her body was smooth and narrow, the buttocks low slung and soft. Her hair was drawn up into a high rubber band, the knots of her backbone rippled down into her waist. She slid open another glass door and stepped into the women's washroom.

It was full of women and children, soaping and washing. Around the pink tiled walls, low near the floor, were a row of taps. Running water gushed noisily. They found two sets of free taps and crouched down, placing the plastic bowls on the floor. Next to Natsuko a woman knelt, her head a lathery mass of shampoo. Beside her a child filled and refilled his bowl, sluicing the water over himself, watching it slap the tiles at his feet. Wet hair plastered his forehead in streaming fingers. From his nose mucus ran into the water. Through the steam bodies gleamed wetly. Natsuko looked over her shoulder and saw the gentle, repeated curve of crouched back after naked back, all pink with warmth and scrubbing. A concentration of soaping and rinsing filled the room. Next to Natsuko now the woman massaged soap up and down her arms, in circular movements over her breasts and stomach, eyes closed. Tight permed curls of wet hair covered her head like wriggling black worms.

Hiroko pulled at her arm impatiently. Taking the soap in her hand Natsuko turned on the taps, mixing water in the bowl, splashing it over her body. Warmth engulfed and relaxed her. Rubbing lather on to her skin she soaped all over. Beside her Hiroko knelt on one knee. Along the inner side of her thigh the skin was white and soft, at the base of her stomach the triangle small and feathery, the breasts nearly flat. Her nakedness did not overpower.

Sometimes Natsuko bathed with her mother. Having seen no other woman naked, she accepted her. But she had not appeared like these slight limbs, flesh tight about their core. On her mother nakedness had overflowed the bones, loose in places, sinewy in others. On the back of her knee spread a web of blue veins, one of them knotted and raised. Across her stomach fatty tissue had the look of dough. There seemed much more to her naked than dressed.

Hiroko was finished. Taking up a bowl of water she threw it over Natsuko. It ran through her hair, blurring her eyes, filling her nostrils so that she spluttered. Hiroko was already opening the next glass door, ready to enter the main bath.

It was bigger than a swimming pool, irregular in shape. Steam breathed off its surface. It was sunken low in the ground, tiled a bright green. The side was rough and rocky, like a grotto. One length of the bath was entirely window, huge and uninterrupted, looking out on to a narrow garden of white raked gravel, rocks and bamboo. Behind the purple hills uncurled. The other length of the bath was banked up with rocks to a mossy stretch of short palm trees. The bath was not crowded, heads dotted the water sparsely. Most of the men sat at the further end with small folded squares of wet towel on top of their heads, to cool them.

The bath was hotter than Natsuko imagined. Around her knees it scalded, the shock goose-pimpling her body. She jumped back to the first step, pulling her feet out in turn. Hiroko was already in, flushed pink beneath the water. Slowly, lowering herself inch by inch she gradually worked her way in. The heat made her dizzy. Sitting on the bottom step beside Hiroko, she leaned her head back on the rocks behind, and stared at the window of tranquil garden. It was all right now. The heat passed right through her body, making her feel too heavy to move. Beneath the water her limbs appeared pale and swollen. When she moved her legs they floated up without effort, as if disconnected. On her lips the condensation of the steam had a caustic taste, filled with the minerals for which the spa was famous.

Propped on her elbows beside Natsuko, Hiroko paddled her legs out in front. Her slight breasts swayed gently, the nipples large pink discs below the surface. Between her legs the soft hair moved weightlessly, like the fronds of weeds. Natsuko kept looking. She remembered the feathery plants around the sides of her grandfather's pond, stirred by the motion of the fish. Hiroko appeared asleep, face tipped back, eyes closed. Natsuko stared without interruption, and soon, what had appeared inviolable became ordinary, even dull. She remembered the naked woman of New Year's Eve, the sudden sob in Riichi's breath, and wondered what it was she could not see. Looking up then, she saw her father.

They must have been sitting there all the time, he and Riichi, some distance away, amongst the men. She waved to them, and tried to get up. But now the heat was too much spiralling up through her in waves, making her feel faint. She pulled herself heavily out of the water. For a moment everything swirled about her. Abruptly she sat down on the top step, head in hands. It passed and she looked up again. Her father was motioning her to leave the water. Below, Hiroko had moved up a step. Her nipples broke the surface, her breasts bobbed gently. She stood and turned, walking up the steps, out of the bath. Kazuo and Riichi watched the water run in streams down her legs and arms, following her back as she walked to the door. Seeing their eyes upon Hiroko's nakedness Natsuko felt a tightening in her chest, and a confusion of feeling she did not understand. It burnt in the steamy air. Looking down at the wet tiles then she saw her own shadow was a spindly rag. Suddenly she wanted to cry.

In Kazuo's room they were served a dinner of fried shrimps, salad, white rice, pickles and bean paste soup. They ate together, sitting on the floor around a low table. Kazuo drank *sake* rice wine, and Hiroko poured it in her usual fashion. But Kazuo was silent and did not speak much.

After the bath Natsuko no longer felt cold. The water had dried from her body almost before she could towel it off. Her flesh was hot and red and cooked. She felt like the octopus Hiroko had lifted from the pot. She ate a good meal. Cleaning the last grain of rice from her bowl, she looked up at Riichi across the table. His eyes were fixed upon Hiroko in a strange glazed way. She was busy eating and did not seem to notice. Quickly Natsuko checked Hiroko's cotton *kimono*, but found it neatly tied, wrapped over demurely, high at the neck. No accidental chink of flesh escaped. Yet Riichi still stared. Tension wound tightly in Natsuko again. The sound of their lacquer chopsticks against the bowls drummed in her head. She kept her eyes upon Hiroko. Only once, as she finished the last mouthful of rice, sucking the chopsticks in her mouth, did Hiroko glance up at Riichi over her bowl. But she looked away quickly, busying herself in the piling of plates.

Getting up from the table they slid back the paper doors beyond the matted section of the room. It opened upon a narrow carpeted strip before the window. Two chairs and a small table looked out over the town. Now the hills were dark, crowding in upon them, the lights of the town heaped in a mass at their base. In the street below groups of people strolled past, identified by the *kimono* of their respective hotels.

'Come,' said Hiroko. 'Leave your father to rest. Let's go down.'

In the lobby Hiroko walked over immediately to a souvenir section, with glass cases of fans and beaded bags. They left her there and went out of the hotel, to the road outside.

The shops were all lit up. Some had no glass fronts and opened directly on to the street. Mostly they sold bric-à-brac souvenirs, plastic toys and edibles. They crossed from the hotel to the shop opposite. There they bought first a tin of flat, round wafer biscuits, for which the town was famous. Munching these they studied the shelves of merchandise. The sweets and kewpie dolls, the gaudy comic books, bath towels with a vanishing naked *geisha*, who only showed when it was wet, miniature dolls of matchsticks and paper, brush ink scrolls and table mats, spilled brightly before them. Riichi became glued to a selection of rocks and minerals, examining carefully the cubic prisms of iron pyrites, feldspar and quartz. Natsuko left him, walking purposefully to the back of the shop.

She had seen the bird from the pavement, staring over glass cases of dolls and polished driftwood sculpture. Only stillness betrayed it was stuffed. It balanced on a mounted wooden branch, head dipped forward, wings spread wide. Flaring out beneath its pale brows amber glass eyes were unforgiving, between them the little beak was sharp as a sickle. The skin on the legs was scaly and yellow, pulled tautly across sinew and bone. One black nailed foot crushed to the branch a dead squirrel, hanging limply, its belly fur pale and soft, its mouth open upon small teeth.

Slowly, holding her breath, Natsuko reached out, touching with the tip of her finger the light speckled breast. The feathers were soft as velvet, melting beneath her. Stretching further she ran a finger along the hard ridge of muscle on the open wing. It was then the bird moved, wobbling slightly, undecided, top heavy on its stand. A picture flashed in her mind of the bird, falling, perch broken, feathers blowing over the floor, the squirrel flung free. Frightened then, she reached out both hands to steady it. Her fingers pushed deeply into the feathers. The beak touched her arm, cold and horny. Under her fingers she felt the hard ungiving body and thought of the insides, drained away, replaced by something that kept it whole long after it was dead. The bird steadied, looking fiercely at her. Heart thumping, Natsuko stepped back. Turning she walked quickly away, searching for Riichi.

He was outside, slipping coins into a bright pink vending machine. Magazines were displayed in its window. With a thud and a rattle change fell out and a magazine dropped down. Riichi picked it up and pushed it hurriedly into the square hanging sleeve of his *kimono*.

'What did you buy?' She could tell he had not expected her. He started, turning.

'Nothing. You're a nuisance. Go away. I'm sick of you, always interfering.' He walked abruptly across the road back into the hotel.

She glanced up at the machine, but its window was in shadow. It was too dark to see clearly, and the magazines did not seem familiar. She followed Riichi across the road.

It was good for us all, Kazuo thought the next evening, after they returned home. He settled himself on the couch in the study and picked up a magazine. The unexpected feelings shared with Riichi pleased him greatly. It was due entirely to Frances' absence, he decided. He realized that he had allowed himself only a superficial wondering about Frances. It was difficult to summon the appropriate concern. He tried to feel guilty, and could not. There had been a cable of safe arrival and two postcards. He had written, briefly, details mostly of the children's welfare, and domestic arrangements. He had yet to receive a reply, and wanted none. He dreaded seeing the neat fall of words upon a page, their tone of accusation and remorse, bringing her to him again. Now, if he tried it was difficult to conjure a clear physical exactness. She came to him in fragments, a walk or a gesture, her hands, the line of her hair, a tone of voice. But her eyes, her expression, the shape of her face defied him completely. In his study, stretched out on the couch, he sank gratefully into this inability, and neither questioned it nor cared. Instead he opened the magazine in his hands haphazardly, at an article upon the Asuka tombs in Nara. And suddenly from the page, the face of the woman Hiroko welled up, each detail clear, the pores of her skin, the loose curve of eyebrow, a few straggled hairs in its arc. He remembered occasions in the last few days when, meeting his gaze fully, she did not lower her eyes. He remembered each time the expression behind her smile. Pressing his knees together, he turned the page abruptly.

She drank her milk in the kitchen, sitting at the table, and looked at the skin formed on top of the liquid in the blue mug. Her mother always fished it off with a spoon before giving it to Natsuko to drink. She sipped again, and it stuck to her lip like wet tissue paper. With her tongue she transferred it to the far rim of the mug. Hiroko was ironing, clothes Kazuo Akazawa would need in the morning. She had set up the ironing board near Natsuko. As she drew the iron across the top it wobbled on its long crossed legs, like an ungainly bird. A yellow and white striped cover tied over the ironing board. Frances had made it to hide scorch marks underneath, with material left from a Summer dress she made Natsuko. And Natsuko remembered now, how she had watched the yellow stripes gather quickly under the needle of the sewing machine, the peeling red ovals of her mother's nails moving closer and closer to the frantic shuttle, escaping just in time. She wanted to ask, when will she come home? Why could I not have gone with her? Why did she have to go at all? Riichi just shrugged when asked and said she was ill without elaboration, waving her angrily from his room. And from her father there would be again the long confusing explanations she did not understand, driving the fear in her deeper.

On the ironing board she watched Hiroko's small hand clasp the black handle of the iron, propelling the weight of chrome back and forth. Nothing would make her ask Hiroko. The clean linen was stacked in a pile on the table, underwear neatly folded, cuffs and fronts of shirts buttoned, concertinaed into rectangles, one on top of another. Her mother hung shirts open and loose upon a hanger, saying she had no time to fuss.

Everywhere Natsuko turned now it was like that, unfamiliar. The house was filled by a small echoing note of strangeness. The arrangement of flowers in an unexpected corner. One of Hiroko's crocheted mats where no mat had been before. The lemony smell from a household deodorant Hiroko sprayed lavishly about, the unbalanced arrangement of bric-à-brac on shelves. Natsuko sensed a fine balance changed. Hiroko protruded everywhere, while her mother sank to the back of cupboards, and settled with the dust.

The milk was nearly finished. Looking down into the deep blue mug, at the froth drying in a fine lather round the sides, she wondered when things would feel all right again. When the thick, dead feeling inside her would lift. Abruptly the mug was pulled from her hand.

'I haven't finished.' She looked up into Hiroko's face. The hair was pulled tightly into a large clip at the back of her head. It drew her eyes up tautly at the corners, accentuating their narrow slant, making her mouth look fat and square.

'It's finished enough. You're just wasting time. Go up to bed, now,' Hiroko said.

She wished she could take stuffed animals to bed, like Riichi when he was much younger. But they never gave her comfort. Instead they grew in the dark and against a night window their ears changed to the shape of bats. Natsuko pulled the quilt into a lump beside her, pressing it under her cheek. She pushed a thumb into her mouth.

It was dark when the door opened quietly, waking her, and after a moment shut again. Her father's footsteps walked away, his bedroom door opened and shut. Now when she woke she did not go to Riichi, fearing his scorn. And in her parents' room was not even the thought of her mother, just an empty side of the bed, and bottles on the dressing-table gathering dust.

A faint light pushed through a gap in the curtains, on to the wall, illuminating a huge papiermâché dragon-fly she had made at school. Her mother insisted they hang it there, proudly. Its ungainly wired blue tissue wings spread several feet across the wall. In a breeze they moved, rustling slightly. The wire edge of the wings, thrusting out determinedly, reminded her of the stuffed hawk, the power in that one strip of muscle. She shivered. Tomorrow the weekend was finished, it was school again. Its rigidities and pressures loomed suddenly at her over the edge of the night. They went to an American missionary school, not far from the house. The children there came mostly with parents on company postings. Within two or three years they moved on. She had three times lost the beginnings of friendship in this way. Now she no longer tried. At breaktimes she sat on the periphery of groups, observing the easy interplay, the loose pitched give and take. There had been conferences about her at school

93

with her parents. Her disinterest and withdrawn attitude had been examined. These criticisms passed diluted to her, she heard them as if of another person. In her mind the clenched grey knot just grew tighter, through it people pushed and pried, laughed at or were angry with her. The school week was filled with the effort of endurance. She was stared at impatiently, with constant urgings to concentrate and work harder. Then, as she looked at words and figures, meanings dissolved, or entered her mind only to be clogged in hedgerows of cotton wool. She wondered if it would ever end. If she would ever do as well as Riichi, whose grades were good and whom friends greeted from across the street.

In her mouth the thumb was soft and pappy. More steps sounded in the corridor outside her room. The door opened, a bar of yellow light pushed in. Through half closed eyes she saw the outline of Hiroko, in her arms a pile of linen. For a moment she stood there silent, light touched the seams and buttons of folded shirts. Then, quietly she pulled the door shut. Her feet padded away to the next room. Natsuko listened to the short knock, to her father's voice, and opening door.

'Put it down there,' he said.

Bending, her back to him she placed the pile of linen on the stool. She rearranged the order of folded underwear and socks to balance the pyramid securely. Behind her he watched. It pleased him, this exactness, this attention to his needs, the crisp folded shirts, the rolled balls of socks, even his underpants ironed. No one had given him such meticulous care since he lived in his parents' house.

She was still attending to the pile, her head bent forward, the hollow of her neck soft and white. It was unnecessary, he

94

knew, to take so long, to rearrange with such care a pile of linen. She was waiting. He was sure of it then, that moment by moment this was what they both had consciously planned. Slowly, he turned to the open door, shutting it quietly, making no noise.

There was only a muffled click, no more. But she was used to listening in the night for unseen things that might reach out for her. She knew with exactness from what part of the corridor a floorboard creaked. Her father's door shut. There was the slight grate of the key. She waited for Hiroko's footsteps to die away. None came. They seemed cut off at the door. She waited thinking they would begin in a moment, flip-flapping away down the passage. Silence. For some reason Hiroko appeared standing in the corridor. Moments passed, but no footsteps came.

Then, from the middle of her stomach the tightening began spreading out until her body was rigid, until her lungs could fill only in short shallow breaths. Hiroko was still in the room. She knew it now. Certainty possessed her. The door was shut and locked. Everything in her knew this was so. The blackness whispered it alive. She sat up then, and waited. Why Hiroko should be in the room, what purpose made it necessary to shut and lock the door, she did not know. She was sure only of these facts holding something more terrible than could be imagined. But the exact cause of this terror was denied her, its reason would not come clear. She was left only with the periphery of emotion.

Shivering began in her then. Her teeth rattled, biting the sides of her tongue, nausea retched emptily in her. She clutched the covers tight in her hand, knees pulled up under her chin. Straining her ears she waited, knowing sooner or later there must be a clue. The silence was alive with sensations, pricking sharp as electricity. Once she thought she heard a whisper, several times a creak of the bed. But nothing more. Nothing. Then suddenly again, a careful opening door. Soft footsteps, silence.

Quickly then she got out of bed and went to the door. Opening it silently, just a crack, she peered out into the passage. The dark was eased by a lamp on the landing of the stairs, left burning at night. Hiroko was not there. But, crouched before Kazuo's door was Riichi, his face pressed to the keyhole. In his body nothing moved.

It seemed they stood a long time, she with her nose to the crack, feet cold and numb, and Riichi, unaware, crouched at their father's door. There was no sound or movement. Only waiting. The silence was filled by her heart, thumping and bumping about in her chest, breaking through into her head, and hammering madly there.

Then, in a quick movement, Riichi started up. She could see his legs were stiff by the awkward way he rose. At the door she moved and he turned his head. She saw then his face was flushed, his eyes bright and disconnected in a way she remembered once when he was ill. He turned and disappeared quickly into his room.

Carefully, she stepped into the passage, walking to her father's door. Bending she pressed her eye to the keyhole. First she saw nothing but a blur of light. Then on the stool the pile of linen, the exact buttoned buttons, the tight balls of socks. A small part of the bed was visible, the sheets drawn back. It was empty and white. She could see nothing of her father. Then a green patch filled the hole. Hiroko was walking towards the door. Natsuko ran quickly back to her room. Leaning against the inside of the door, she heard at last the sound of Hiroko's feet, flip-flapping away down the stairs.

Long after the shivering stopped she lay tossing, unable to settle. Her limbs refused to lie calmly between the sheets. She did not sleep until the first grey light filtered through the curtains on to the tissue wings of the dragon-fly, making it diaphanous, so that she could see upon the wall behind the strings and pins that held it there.

[7]

Riichi said nothing. He doubled over the slice of toast, marmalade oozed between the crusts. A dollop dropped on to the table. He scooped it up with a finger, licking it off. Eating, he bit large chunks, chewed distractedly, bit again too soon, stuffing it all into his mouth, hardly tasting.

Natsuko could not eat. Exhaustion filled her. Something had happened last night, she did not know what. The churning feelings tired her out, she was an old woman, weathered and bent. She searched for words to fetter sensations. Rootless, without name or identity they swam unheedingly in her, knocking at her nerves. But from Riichi she sensed a strange new energy, jerking about, filling him hotly. He could not sit still. His eyes followed Hiroko about the kitchen, as she moved from sink to stove. Natsuko knew the old balances were gone, irretrievably. This room, beyond it the house, the people in it, were separated from her. From now she would only drift, extraneously through it. Everything was soured and treacherous. This much she understood. It had begun with Hiroko.

Abruptly Riichi stood up, swinging his school bag over his arm. He was going before Natsuko this morning, he had a project at school to revise. Half an hour was left before Natsuko need leave. Upstairs her father was getting dressed, she heard the slam of the bathroom door. She sipped hot milk, nose deep in the mug. Steam rose in a circle to the centre of her face. Before her the cereal was untouched. The thought of eating made her sick. Finishing the milk she took the empty mug to the sink. With a soapy sponge Hiroko was washing Riichi's plate.

'Have you finished?'

'I don't want any breakfast.'

'No. You must eat. You can't waste all that food.' Hiroko sounded annoyed.

'But, I don't want it.' Natsuko heard her own voice shouting the words. At once Hiroko whipped around, eyes narrowed. In the sink she let go of the plate and sponge, and took hold of Natsuko's arm.

The hand was warm and wet on Natsuko. A skin of soapy bubbles slid from Hiroko's fingers on to Natsuko's arm, and dribbled down to her elbow.

'You'll eat if it makes you sick. You'll learn to do as you're told.' Hiroko began pulling Natsuko back to the table.

Tugging the other way, afraid of being struck, Natsuko looked down and saw Hiroko's feet in open-backed slippers. The front of her foot was lost beneath green felt. Only the heel and ankle were visible, thick and strong. Soft wrinkles of stocking encircled them. The muscles were straining and pulling, the heel digging obstinately into the floor. Suddenly it seemed everything Natsuko hated was in those feet. She remembered the legs flung out on the bed, one foot over a pile of her mother's clothes, and the obnoxious flip-flapping that followed her everywhere. Hiroko gave an extra hard push, and the edge of the table came up hard against Natsuko's hip. She saw Hiroko raise her hand. Bending backwards then, Natsuko kicked out as hard as she could.

It surprised her most to feel substance, the wall of bone and flesh, stopping her foot. Hiroko cried out and immediately let go of Natsuko. She thought, 'I have done it. I kicked her.'

The pleasure of it was warm. She turned and ran, leaving Hiroko rubbing her shin.

In the hallway she picked up her school bag and fled out of the door. Once, at the gate, she stopped, expecting Hiroko somewhere behind. But she was not to be seen. The windows of the house were free of her face, staring outward, non-committal. Beyond the gate a breeze rustled through tall, dry grass. A swift darted up and flew away. She turned and began the walk to school.

It was a relief to be out of the house. Walking the narrow curving road descending the hill, she pushed her toes down hard, leaning back with her body to balance the steeper parts. From the side she pulled off a blade of grass, rubbing it in her fingers, smelling the sharp juicy smell on her hands. It was warm and sunny. Taking off her cardigan she tied it by the sleeves about her waist, stretching her arms, feeling the sun on her skin. She pulled again at a shrub and a butterfly rose up. They were beginning now, every day she saw one or two little white cabbage butterflies. Spring would soon be early Summer. Already cherry blossom petals clogged the gutters, mixing with orange juice cans and paper bags. Along the side of the road pollen from catkins of an overhanging tree was trampled like a green velvet patch into the surface of the road. Everything was better in Summer, they lived less in the house, more in the garden. And even then, doors and windows were flung open. Warmth, if not sun, pushed into the dark rooms.

Even at the most ordinary times she felt in their house something strange and inexplicable. It was an old house. At night Natsuko lay sometimes and thought of the people who had lived there before them. She wondered if anyone had died there, especially in her own room. With her mother absent these apprehensions attacked her more often, shapeless, dark and menacing. They hovered just below her skin, breathing softly on her nerves.

The night before she had woken, thirsty, and gone to the bathroom for a drink of water. She cupped her hand under the tap and drank. Still half asleep, she turned to go back to bed, into the passage outside the bathroom. It was not dark, on the upper landing was the light they left on at night. But Natsuko had glanced over her shoulder, down the well of the staircase and had seen the blackness at the bottom. At once all drowsiness left her. She stood, rigid, looking down into the ring of night. It filled her with terror, for she saw the house did not sleep with them. The blackness was alive, staring back at her, waiting. If she dared to go down it would consume her. She ran back to her room, heart thumping. No light, no locked door could ever deter the secret life within the house.

Other people's houses were not like this. She knew, for once, briefly, she had a friend at school, an American girl called Suzanne, who had left to go on to Jakarta. Sometimes she visited Suzanne's home, a modern flat by a traffic light in the middle of Kobe. There had been six floors to the block, and a fast lift up and down. The walls and floors of the entrance hall were of polished stone. There were bells to ring and a microphone at street level, to speak directly to the flats above. Suzanne's apartment was sun, light and plant-filled balconies. The ceilings were low and smooth, the walls untroubled. They ate cake and cheese sandwiches in the kitchen. It was all plastic, chrome and press button gadgets. Suzanne showed her how even the rubbish was ground up by a machine in the sink, and flushed away down the water pipe. She pushed in egg shells, a cabbage leaf, left-over sandwiches and a paper bag to demonstrate. With a terrible rattle everything vanished, pulverized to dust while Natsuko watched. Suzanne's bedroom was a small neat box, the windows light and chrome edged, unlike the cumbersome wooden-framed windows of Natsuko's own room, that must be opened by an adult. One wall was a brilliant green and everything else, furniture, curtains, ornaments matched in either green or white. There were clown dolls to put pyjamas into hanging on the walls. In one corner of the floor a family of patchwork turtles made a flowery green and pink tower. In the lounge after tea Suzanne's mother, dressed in black leotards, practised yoga on a floor of cushions. Smilingly, she invited them to join her. They had tried, rolling and laughing over the cushions. A small, soft-haired dog called George romped with them, jumping and barking. Whenever he could he licked Natsuko's face with his soft, moist tongue.

Before going home Natsuko looked from the window of Suzanne's bedroom and saw the building opposite, filled with lighted frames. In each, people and activities went on, like many separate plays. In the road below cars and buses passed. Here, it seemed, nobody was ever alone. She thought enviously of Suzanne, able to wake in the middle of the night, and look from the window at the lights of other people.

Suzanne's mother drove Natsuko home. It was dusk as they approached the house. Tall trees stood darkly around it, melting into one another, ominously. The windows were tight lipped and disapproving. She wished she need never come back. That night she thought about it all and knew everything would always be all right, could she live in the chrome-filled, white-walled flat of Suzanne. But now that seemed a long time ago. Her life would always be different. It did not contain the airy space, the pyjama dolls or the turtle family of Suzanne. She knew now it never would.

In spite of the sun, a haze shrouded the bay, and came down like a white sheet to the edge of the Kobe docks. Sea, sky and Wakayama were all hidden. The haze rose up like a wide blank canvas. Walking down the hill Natsuko had several times run her finger over the letter in her pocket. At the bottom she sat on a low wall to read it again.

It was a blue airmail letter form, thin and crisp. She held the smoothness between her fingers looking at her own name written there, in her mother's small neat writing. It was not long.

Darling,

I have thought and thought about you all, wondering how you are. I really am so worried. I do hope Hiroko has turned out all right, and that she is managing the cooking. Are you eating enough? I don't think it can yet be too warm, so don't forget to take at least a cardigan to school with you. Even on a warm day it can turn chilly suddenly in the middle of the afternoon. And that, of course, is just the moment you can catch a cold.

Don't worry about me. I am resting and taking lots of medicine to try and feel better. The doctor is good and kind but it will take a little while longer before I am well enough to return. Be brave. Be a very good girl for Daddy and Hiroko. Do everything they tell you. It will be a great help to me if you do.

With lots of love,
Mummy

She had some trouble in places following the writing. Her father had read it with her and then she understood. But the meaning made no difference. She looked at the date, written a week ago, and found it made no sense. For a few moments, writing these words, sitting thousands of miles away, her mother had thought briefly of her, one week ago. Sitting on a stone wall at the bottom of the hill, one week later, it did not apply. Her mother lived now in a different time, a different dimension. She might as well be dead. She was not here, she could not be touched, seen or spoken to. She could only be written to and, in one week's time, she would read the words put down by Natsuko on a piece of paper. The uselessness of it all made her want to cry. She had waited for this letter, but understanding its form now, she felt even more alone than before. Suddenly, angrily, she shredded the letter into little bits. Twisting round on the wall she dropped it all into the open drain behind her, filled with the water of mountain streams. She watched the little bits of blue confetti stick to the moving surface and ride away. One piece swam safely to the stones at the side and rested there. From it the words stared up at Natsuko, surrounded by their ragged edge: Hiroko, enough. I. cardigan.

'Listen,' he said, and began to read to them from the book. 'Note on the game of playing football: The game of football was in great favour at the Japanese court. It was introduced from China in the seventh century. The Emperor Mommu, who reigned at the end of that century, was the first emperor to take part in the sport. His majesty Toba the second became very expert at it, as also did the noble Asukai Chirjo, and from that time a sort of football club was formed at the palace. During the days of extreme poverty of the Mikado and his court the Asukai family, notwithstanding their high rank, were wont to eke out their scanty income by giving lessons in the art of playing football.'

Kazuo looked over his book at Riichi, and they both laughed. They had just returned from a baseball game. At the stadium the Yomiuri Giants had played the Hankyu Braves. Natsuko had not gone. She listened to them talking excitedly of the number of home runs, the fantastic pitching of the star player, the unbeatable brilliance of the favourite team. Nowadays they did a lot of things together that left her alone at home.

In the evenings now it had become a ritual that they sat with him in the study. He read or talked about all kinds of diverse historical facts. Mostly she was bored, except when he read the fairy stories. Of these there was one each night. Tales of vampire cats, foxes that changed into beautiful women, badgers who lured victims by drumming upon bloated stomachs, a boy born from a peach. Some of these she already knew, others not. But he was finished now with the famous Cat of Nabashima, a two-tailed vampire monster. Now he would send her to bed. It was so each night. After the door was shut he and Riichi talked on.

'Natsuko you should go to bed. Riichi will be up later.' When she came to him he kissed her, relieved to see her docile. At least in the evenings he was sure the adjustment was right. A traditional story for Natsuko, and then he could turn to Riichi. It was difficult to know how long Frances might stay away. Once she returned the flow between himself and Riichi would surely be disrupted. It was important to lay a foundation quickly. The abhorrence Frances generated for certain aspects of Japanese life was absurdly out of context. He wanted desperately for Riichi to respect and understand the code of ethics, the courage and dignity behind much of what Frances ridiculed. Now they were reading from Lord Redesdale's book, his historical Western view. With this he alternated from his own long article on the Samurai ethical code. Riichi listened intently, Kazuo was pleased.

Outside the door Natsuko paused. They were reading of ceremonial *hara kiri* executions long ago. Last night all she heard were the boring details of etiquette. That the execution place must be eighteen feet square, at what angle the condemned man should sit, how many quilts he should sit on, of what colour and order they should be, what clothes the witnesses should wear, what clothes the seconds should wear, how high when sitting they may hitch their trousers.

'. . . afterwards the head is to be struck off at one blow. To lay down thick paper and place the head upon it shows a disposition of respect to the head. To place it on the edge of the sword is insulting. The course pursued must depend on the rank of the person . . .' Her father read. Natsuko shivered and ran upstairs.

Before Riichi's room she hesitated, then slipped in, closing the door. She had thought of it suddenly and knew it must be somewhere. She remembered the size, a vague pattern of colours. On the bookshelves was nothing like it, only firmly bound books and martial art magazines. The drawers of the desk and the cupboard produced nothing. Kneeling she looked under the bed. There was a baseball glove, a battered cardboard box and thick rolls of dust. She pulled out the box, angry at all the secrets, cutting her off. It seemed they all, her father, Riichi and Hiroko, were no more than a myriad of little drawers, in each a thought, a feeling, a piece of knowledge. Sometimes these drawers were opened and the contents shared. At those times Natsuko saw threads of emotion vibrate briefly between the three of them. But these warm and vital communications were never extended to her.

Pulling open the flaps of the box, she saw it staring at her, the magazine Riichi had bought in Arima. She picked it up, beneath on a pile of comics Superman struggled with a horned monster. But it was the smooth, polished limbs of a scantily dressed woman that trembled in her hands. She was afraid, kneeling beside the box, that Riichi might soon come up. Furtively, she opened the magazine. It did not take long to absorb the essentials, flicking quickly through the pages.

Afterwards she replaced it carefully, but her heart was thumping, and her stomach tight in the same way as when the *kimono* had fallen from the spindly body of the dancer on New Year's Eve. But above these feelings, as she pushed the box back under the bed to its resting place amongst the dust, came anger for Riichi. As she closed the door behind her it knifed up, filling her mind with the pictures she had seen, the raised arms and legs, the taut thrusting midriffs, and soft globes of breast.

Lying on her bed she began to cry, until her head throbbed and her nose was full and clogged, unable to understand the confusions around her. They plaited into a thick weaving stem, and from them she could extract and claim not a single strand.

'It will not be for long, just over the weekend. It is kind of Hiroko to take you with her.' Kazuo worked with his tongue at a piece of pork cutlet stuck between teeth. Across the table Natsuko watched the moving lump in his cheek. He was going to Tokyo, Riichi would accompany him. There was an important exhibition of swords and scrolls of famous battles they were interested to see. Once Kazuo's appointment with his publisher was over they would have time for this and much more. It would have been enough, thought Natsuko, to have stayed here, alone with Hiroko. But a telephone call had come the day before, telling Hiroko her mother was ill. Natsuko could neither be taken to Tokyo nor left alone. It had been decided she would go with Hiroko, back to her village home.

'Hiroko's village is famous for handmade paper. Her family are papermakers. There will be much of interest there for you to see.' Kazuo wiped grease from his mouth on the corner of a paper napkin.

In her own mouth the lump of meat was rubbery and fibrous. Natsuko rolled it about, unable to swallow. The voices of Riichi and her father swung back and forth across the table, planning, timing, anticipating. Riichi's manner was excited, Kazuo smiled expansively. Their journey was already begun.

The tablecloth spread before Natsuko, white and blank. On plates a film of grease congealed. It was useless to protest. Day by day a strange feeling grew in her. She was shrinking. Her limbs were heavy and would not move quickly. When she wished to speak no voice came. It was worst inside her head. There everything was blanketed by opacity, thoughts and feelings loomed through only vaguely. As she tried to grasp them they disintegrated and were lost. Everything seemed a dream, floating beyond reach. Nothing appeared real. Looking down she saw her hands, the white half moon at the base of each nail, the edge of the tablecloth upon her knees. These things must be believed. If she bit her tongue it hurt. She appeared in the mirror as always. It was impossible to explain the feeling inside her, the tightening and blurring, the growing smaller hour by hour. Sometimes she looked up suddenly and things were double their size. A chair became too huge to sit on, mouths and eyes engorged filling a face, pushing out all else. Coming towards her, to touch or take, hands appeared first soft, then as they neared, fixed and crabby like claws, and dangerous, to be avoided.

Expressions changed in the same appalling way. What appeared a smile became a grimace of teeth, saliva and tongue. There was nothing left to trust. She saw each day rotting in her, hopeless. And beyond was nowhere to run to. Even night now ceased to plunge her into its black emptiness. Sleep was fitful and never deep. Strange noises slid off the night and the walls of the house, and always now were the soft opening and shutting of doors, the whispers and rustles, the creak of the bed in rhythmic spasms. She no longer crept out to search the meaning, to see if Riichi still crouched at the keyhole. She pulled the covers over her ears, and drew her knees tight to her belly, in an effort to stop the shivering.

[8]

It was a fine Saturday morning. They left first, walking down the hill to the station. Hiroko carried a canvas bag, Natsuko a small blue knapsack on her back. They took the train, changing once. The first was crowded, taking commuters to the busy centre of Osaka. They stood all the way, swaying precariously, hemmed in so tightly by bodies they could not fall. Natsuko clung to Hiroko's hand, staring at jacket ends, handbags and hips. Sometimes she glimpsed a chink of window and through it T.V. aerials, scaffolding, washing, the cross-hatching of tiled roofs, a continuous harsh grey texturing each side of the train. Conversation filled the racks, hot air blew up beneath her feet. A printed ribbon of newspapers, spread wide before seats, folded to convenient squares by strap-hanging commuters, wove in and out the length of the carriage. The second train was comparatively empty. Natsuko sat on an olive plush seat, glad to breathe freely and look about. Now they had begun to leave the town. The grey depression of factories and concrete broke gradually, giving way to a patchwork farmland. Fallow paddy fields cut to a stubble, the neat lines of turnips and cabbages snuggled close to the ground. They passed an electric generator, all springs and pylons, a school playground alive with blue tracksuits, a mass of parked bicycles before a station, mercurial in a sudden pool of sun. White and ultramarine, the bullet train streaked by on a track below them, on the way to Tokyo. Then, in the distance, the dark olives and umbers of tree-covered hills moved nearer, pale feathery slabs of bamboo at the base. The crusty tiled roofs of houses looked cleaner, windows brighter. A sequence of new houses still showed raw wood skeletons, a temple with a large bronze bell hanging from its deep eaves rushed by. In the train Natsuko looked at the bright advertisements hanging like flags from special hooks in the ceiling, glossy colour spots of *Kabuki*, fashions, red-lipped girls and slabs of chocolate. A microphone announced each station, echoing down the carriage. Sometimes, swinging deliriously round a curve, Natsuko saw the front of the train through a window, snaking ahead of them. Next to her a young girl studied a book of English lessons, another in a black coat and high boots, stood nearly in front of her, carrying a cased violin. Beside the door an elderly woman swayed unsteadily, clutching two long-stemmed bunches of flowers for an arrangement lesson. The head of each chrysanthemum was swathed in tissue paper. Above a short coat her mauve scarf picked out the colour of her *kimono* and the flowers. Time passed quickly, and Hiroko, equally absorbed did not bother with Natsuko, and only spoke to tell her they had reached their station.

The bus was empty but for a farmer, a student in black uniform and an old woman in a grey suit, spectacles and an anxious expression. Hiroko and Natsuko sat near the back. Over the empty seats was the rigid, uniformed back of the driver. Natsuko took the inside of the seat, next to the window. Beside her was the warmth of Hiroko's body, from behind the knapsack pushed her forward uncomfortably. She felt suddenly tired and leaned her head against the window. Wherever she looked were tall tree-covered slopes. The road wound up and down and around the contours. Once she saw they were high, the side of the road slipped precipitously away through the vertical strata of conifer trees and bamboo, down over terraced paddy fields to a thin white river far below. Soon again the land was flat, cultivated each side of the bus, the conical hills a distance away in mauve shadow.

Natsuko had woken that morning with a headache. Now the journeying and staring from windows, filled with unfamiliar views pulled the pain tighter in her head. Her eyes hurt when she moved them. Her throat was beginning to feel rough and sore. Beside her Hiroko was unzipping the canvas bag and taking out a plastic box. Inside was their lunch of *onigiri*, cold rice balls wrapped in papery strips of seaweed, two cans of juice and an orange each. Natsuko ate without appetite, turning her face to the window again. In places now trees stood thickly at the side of the road, and against them the window turned dark and reflective. It showed Hiroko's profile behind her, the wide lower jaw moving rhythmically, the thick lips sinking deeply into the soft ball of rice. Then the window grew lighter leaving only Natsuko's own eyes, floating amongst passing fields and hills. The sun shone warmly on the glass. She felt drowsy, and tried not to think of the weekend to come, or the discomfort of the headache.

The bus dropped them outside a garage, red, white and blue, shiny with posters of cars and bikini-clad girls. Around it was silence and strawberry fields, the long furrows of plants blanketed under polythene. Here and there a few leaves pushed above the shroud. Beside the strawberry patches were fallow rice fields, prickly with dry yellow stubble. Natsuko remembered her mother once teasing her, saying the stubble was noodles growing.

Around them the steep hills were a wall, wherever she looked, dark green with coniferous trees. Hiroko was walking forward now, pointing to a narrow road between a cluster of farmhouses, disappearing round a bend. It kept close to the side of a hill, bamboo bent pliantly above, ruffling up in the breeze. The opposite side of the lane were farm workers' houses, some dilapidated with open gardens and fruit trees, others small and closed behind stone walls. Between the road and the hill a narrow strip of land was planted with Japanese mushrooms, grown on straddled logs. Hiroko, suddenly good humoured, told Natsuko how the starchy water of washed rice was poured over the logs each day to ferment and grow the mushrooms. They sprouted like pale nobbly warts all over the wood.

After a while the road met the curve of a river, houses either side of it. The river lay very low, a long way down from the edge of the road and the houses. Its sides were reinforced by a pebbling of stone and concrete. The bed was a series of massive steps, breaking the steep descent of the river. It was empty and dry, overgrown by flowering weeds. At one side a narrow flow of water managed to trickle over the rubble of stones and shrubs. Children played down there, holding fishing rods in the water. A rusted pushchair lay on its side, old shoes and tyres, a wooden box and household remnants were littered about. They walked on beside the river, following the white guard rail at the side of the road, above the steep drop. At a narrow bridge Hiroko turned sharp left, up the slope of a hill.

There was no gate. They turned off the narrow road abruptly, into an opening between trees. The farmhouse stretched before them, old and ramshackle. The roof was thatched a metre thick, eaves reaching deeply over the sides of the house. The sliding wooden window shutters were all closed. A small truck and four bicycles were parked against one wall. At the end of the house bamboo logs piled in a high mound, their hollow ends a honeycomb of dark holes. Where they stood a two-storey modern outhouse was added to the main thatched building. From its second floor washing hung thickly on a rough wooden balcony. An earthen courtyard lay in front of the old house, in it a pond, a few short trees and a forest of potted shrubs. Hiroko walked straight to the main door. Natsuko followed, glancing over her shoulder at the pond. It was murky, the water floating with scum and leaves. She thought she saw the bright red shadow of a fish. Then they passed under the deep eaves of the house, and through the door Hiroko drew back.

Inside it was dark. She stumbled against Hiroko. There seemed at first nothing about her but dim, cavernous space. Then, way above she saw a small patch of light, through a smoke hole in the roof. It filtered on to the scaffolding of beams, crossing and recrossing in deep empty space beneath the roof. The huge rafters were badly warped, blackened by soot and age. Her eyes were growing accustomed to the dimness now. She made out a curved, white tiled hearth, waist high, with great rusted iron cauldrons sunken into its broad top, abandoned long before. To the right it was lighter, there was a small window, a sink, a range of gas burners and refrigerator. Along one wall of the kitchen stood several large earthenware jars of pickles, fermenting in yeasty rice bran. They filled the air with a sour pungency. To the left was a high wooden step up into the living section of the house, and a wall of paper doors. Hiroko stepped up, leaving her shoes on the earthen floor, and slid back a door. Behind was a rush-matted *tatami* room, and people.

An old woman lay between quilts in the middle of the room. Everyone else sat on the floor around her. As Hiroko came in they looked up and greeted her, making a place beside the bed. Natsuko knelt down behind Hiroko. The room was small, partitioned off by another wall of paper doors. Natsuko's cramped toes touched the door behind her. She was kneeling uncomfortably on a hard, covered join between mats. She could barely move; crowded in about her were Hiroko's relatives and neighbours. It was dim in this room too. The window shutters were drawn, except for a slim gap in one. From this light spread halfheartedly, through a thin paper shutter. It was difficult to believe there was sun outside. They had entered a twilight world.

Hiroko's mother lay motionless between the quilts, she seemed asleep. Her skin was flaccid and soft. It slid loosely over the bones of her face, falling into pouches beside her mouth and beneath her chin. The thick double fold of eyelid reminded Natsuko of Hiroko. Age in the woman was not of dryness and wrinkles, it was the feeling of old elastic. Saliva dribbled from the corner of her mouth. At regular intervals a woman bent forward and dabbed it with a tissue.

They sat for a long time. Natsuko's legs grew stiff and numb. About her people talked of the old woman, the details of her illness. Something festered, eating away at her from inside. Nothing could be done. Another operation would be useless. As they spoke the woman stirred and moaned, eyes still closed. She turned suddenly on her side, heaving the quilts with her. Her hand crept along the edge of the upper one, and gripped the white cover. The bones were thin and small, the skin a loose, wrinkled glove. Over its top a raised mesh of veins resembled the long gnarled roots of an old tree. She settled with a sigh. The woman who had dabbed at her mouth leaned forward again, tugging the quilts back into place, meeting the corners exactly, one upon the other.

The door slid back behind Natsuko, someone stepped over

her feet. A young girl carried in a tray of tea bowls. Natsuko reached up at her turn and took one. Blue patterned and squat, the bowl filled her cupped hands, its warmth spreading into her fingers. She looked through the clear green liquid to dots of sediment and a grain of puffed rice that had escaped the spout of the pot. She drank and it was good, light and hot against the dryness of her throat. Someone else came in with a large aluminium kettle and refilled the bowls. Around the sick woman everyone changed positions, drew back, relaxed and began to talk of other things. Suddenly, remembering then, Hiroko turned and told Natsuko she might go outside.

For a moment daylight dazzled her eyes. The air was sweet after the stale body smells and fermenting pickles. She took long breaths, walking to the pond. It reminded her of water left in a bowl after dishwashing, thick and opaque. Leaves and unbroken bubbles drifted over the surface. Dimly beneath she saw the bodies of fish. A long-legged insect sat astride a bubble, flew up and realighted elsewhere on the water. The back of the pond met a bank of small trees against the wall of the next house. The other three sides of the pond were massed with an army of potted shrubs and *bonsai* trees. Row after row, they crowded the ground or stood in tiers on wooden racks. A few of the *bonsai* grew free of pots, clinging to large stones. Their long roots crept down like claws, gripping the moss-covered stone, above their trunks were weathered and bent. Natsuko crouched down, running her finger over their knotted spindly roots and tiny leaves. She looked at the profusion of larger trees behind the pond, at their round flat leaves, restless in the breeze, and then back to the little potted goblins, stunted and miniaturized. It was as if their spirits had been forced back into a narrow tunnel, to be viewed through the wrong end of a telescope.

Looking at them pictures came to her of all manner of midget freak or hunchbacked gnome. She wished suddenly they would all rear up, out of their incarceration, breaking their pots, filling the garden with huge revengeful trunks and branches.

Thinking this, dipping her fingers in the pond, she saw a man's feet appear suddenly beside her. They wore the foot covering of labourers, a dark blue, cleft-toed canvas sock. It hooked tightly up the leg to the calf, the cleft seamed up the middle of the foot. It appeared more an animal hoof than a human limb. The end of the toes were beginning to fray, grey with dust and mud. A nail bulged tautly under the cloth. The feet did not move. Natsuko drew her finger from the water, a thin slime clung over the wetness. Turning her head she looked up. He had not been among the people in the room. She would have remembered the squat face, the small eyes nearly hidden between a cliff of brow and bulging cheekbones. They were like currants, pushed deep into a bun. His skin was brown and weathered against the narrow white towel that was tucked into the collar of his maroon sweater.

Without speaking, he squatted down beside her. Leaning forward he pushed his hand deep into the water, until it rose up high around his arm. Then, pulling out his hand he smiled again, opening his clenched fist near Natsuko's face. In his square palm was a glutinous mass of frog spawn. Within each slimy cell of jelly was the black, squirming body of a tadpole. Still without speaking, but nodding agreeably, he thrust his palm nearer. Hesitantly, Natsuko put out a finger. It was clammy and cold, she drew back quickly. He tipped his hand then, and it slid in a mucousy lump back into the water. Wiping his hand on the back of his trousers he stood up, and silently beckoned. Natsuko followed him along the narrow flagged path, to the back of the pond. There he stopped, bending forward, searching for something among the tall blades of iris leaves, parting the stems carefully. Then he turned, motioning her to come and look. She walked over and stood beside him. At first she saw nothing, for the toad was half hidden under a stone. Then it moved and she saw the small stout body, the colour of soil. The glassy eyes looked at her, the thin membrane beneath its chin dilated and throbbed. Suddenly it jumped. The body flicked upwards like a muddy pebble, and she started back so abruptly she stumbled. He put out a hand steadying her. The red, rough knuckles clasped about her arm, the fingers ingrained with dirt. Over his wrist short black hairs lay flat and wet. He smiled again, and the warmth of his breath touched her face. Revulsion welled up in her. Pulling free she ran back again towards the house. Before she reached the door Hiroko came out, carrying their bags.

'There is no room for us in the house. We'll have to sleep above the workshop.' Hiroko stopped as she saw the man. Tilting her head to one side she gave a small bow, smiling coquettishly. Turning she walked to the workshop, smiling again over her shoulder.

Natsuko followed her into the newer building adjoining the old thatched house. It was cool and damp after the warm sun. The small room was bare except for bundles of dark-skinned shrubs heaped about the walls. An elderly woman in baggy-legged, blue patterned peasant trousers, a white scarf about her head, sat on a stool in the middle of the room. She greeted Hiroko. A mound of the shrubs was loose at her feet, the stems wet and shiny like twisting snakes. With a short knife she peeled off the black bark, stripping it quickly from the white inner stems. In her hand the knife went backwards and forwards, the small curved blade glinting in the light, loose skins curling in a pile at her feet. Nearby a huge metal vat balanced on a great gas burner. A blue ring of flame licked the base, from its open mouth steam unravelled. Boiling in the vat was the basis of paper, the white *gampi* shrubs and a residue of wood ash. Later hibiscus root glue and mud soil were added. Hiroko had grudgingly explained this much on the bus. A blue gas pipe snaked away across the floor to a point in the wall, from it heat radiated fiercely. The peasant woman's face was shiny with sweat, and as they passed near the air was hot in Natsuko's mouth. There was another room opening off into the back, but Hiroko passed this and walked to a ladder of open planks, reaching up to a square opening in the ceiling. She began swinging herself up in an easy rhythm. Natsuko slipped her knapsack on her back, so that both hands were free. Holding on to the side struts she began to climb, careful not to look down between the open spaces of the steps. Near the ceiling she felt like a crawling fly, the room seemed a long way beneath her. The peasant woman was all fore-shortened, a flat head and scarf with hands and blue knees sticking out of it. The boiling vat of shrub pulp was under Natsuko now, she looked straight down into it. Rising up from it, steam settled damply on the backs of her hands and bare legs. Quickly she turned her eyes up, to the ceiling. It was very bright above, after the dank room below. For a moment she felt this must be like entering Heaven. Then she was there, heaving herself on all fours, into the room.

It was large, covering both the rooms downstairs. The centre was matted and clean, but about the wall oddments were thickly stacked. Towers of empty baskets, boxes crammed with dirty roots and rocks, newspapers, rags, and an old spinning wheel, balanced upon two large cans. In the middle of the room, pulled to one side were paper doors. They could be drawn together to divide the room. There were two windows, one looking down into the road to the river, and the other on to a balcony of washing. Between aprons, shirts and underwear, the thatch showed through. The triangular gable end was filled with plaited wood, the high central ridge crossed with bundles of reed and slats. The thatch looked very near, stubbly as the back of a bristling animal. Its shape was like a helmet over the meagre house below. It was not unlike one of the helmets upon the armour in her father's study, thought Natsuko, staring at it through the window. Beyond the thatch down in the yard, she could see the man, loitering still by the pond.

'Who is he?' she asked.

'Only Shojiro. He has been here for years.' Hiroko pulled a face at the window.

'Is he one of your family?'

'He's related to my brother-in-law in a distant way. But what do you want to know all this for? Why are you so interested in Shojiro?' asked Hiroko.

Natsuko remembered the curranty eyes and swallowed the words in her mouth. But without waiting for an answer Hiroko pushed in front of her, opening the window. Climbing out on to the balcony she began to gather up the washing. From below Shojiro watched her. The white starched sleeves of aprons and shirts stuck out stiffly from her arms at awkward angles, as if she carried severed limbs. Piled up against her chest, chin pressing down upon the pile, she climbed back in and dumped the load upon the floor.

'Now, they have quilts for us to sleep on in the cupboard there.' Hiroko pointed to the smooth paper doors that made one wall of the room. Near the floor whiteness was broken by a dark blue band with gold speckled clouds upon it. Sliding back a door, Hiroko pulled out the quilts.

'There is a lot to be done in the house. I've no time for any nonsense from you. Lay out the quilts, and stay up here until I call you. Dinner will not be long. If you don't behave I shall punish you. There will be nobody here to help you,' said Hiroko, her vicious self again, heaving the quilts out on to the floor.

'These are the uppers, these are the lower ones. Lay them out there, behind the divider. The pillows are in the cupboard.' There still remained another set of quilts. Hiroko hesitated, then pulled them out also.

'These must be Shojiro's.' She dragged them across the floor to the other side of the room, and pulled shut the paper divider, cutting the room in two. Then she was gone, disappearing down the stair shaft. There was a small grating sound as she pushed her feet into her wooden clogs, at the bottom of the steps, then the clatter of them across the cement floor. Silence.

Natsuko turned to the quilts, they were heavy and cumbersome, especially the firmly packed lower ones. Bending and heaving at them she felt again the throbbing in her head, the dry irritation in her throat. But at last they were in place, side by side in white coverlets, like two neat envelopes. She reached into the cupboard for the bean pillows. A warm musty smell surrounded her head. It was deep enough to crawl inside. Stretching in she managed to pull out the two small pillows, and placed one on each bed.

Then there was nothing to do. She did not dare go down. Wandering round the room she examined the dusty weaving of the baskets, and the old spinning wheel. Then, pulling back the window she bent, squeezing through it, out on to the balcony.

There were gaps between the wooden planks of the floor, she could see the ground below her. The thatch of the main house was very near here, thick and bristly. Hanging on to a supporting strut of balcony, leaning out as far as she could, the tips of her fingers just grazed the stubble. It was hard as packed wire, scratchy on her fingertips. In that position, her neck tense, the throb beat again in her head, making her feel suddenly sick. She drew back and leaned for a moment upon the upright post, pressing her forehead against the wood. Looking down through the gaps in the floor, she saw them then.

They were standing beneath her, half under the eaves of the old house. Hiroko and the man in the maroon sweater. At first she saw no more than a fragment of their bodies, and the sound of Hiroko's broken laughter. Then they moved directly under the balcony. Through the slats she looked down on the tops of their heads. Hiroko laughed again.

'Get away. Don't be a nuisance. Is this the time?' She gave Shojiro a push. Her fingers spread, small and pale upon his red chest. The man stepped closer, his arm came up abruptly, like a short red bar, level with Hiroko's breast. He reached out and squeezed the soft swell there. Against the white blouse his hand was a great spread legged insect, ugly and thick. But Hiroko only laughed coarsely, and pushed him off again. The arm fell back, the hand disappeared. And from Shojiro came not words but a series of gobbled sounds and grunts. They congealed grotesquely beneath the balcony, half animal, half human. Natsuko felt them slipping through the gaps under her feet, pricking at her skin. Below her Shojiro turned and walked quickly into the workshop. Laughing to herself, Hiroko disappeared beneath the eaves.

Slowly Natsuko climbed back through the window into the room. Shojiro was downstairs now. Pushing up from below his presence crept through her. She waited for the noise of his feet on the stairs, his strange gobbled sounds still in her ears. For several moments she stood by the window, but he did not come. She relaxed a little then, and carefully walked to the stair shaft. Kneeling she could see no further than the bottom step. But, stretching out on her stomach, she was able to curl her head around the opening, into the room below. It was empty, the old woman was gone. Only the vat simmered quietly above the blue ring of flame and a hiss of gas. She could see nothing of Shojiro but, from the room behind, came a rhythmic swish and slap, he was working there. She pulled back from the stair shaft relieved.

Thinking it might ease the pain in her head, she lay down upon the quilts. The linen was soft and coarse under her cheek, warm from the sun through the window, it gave off the musty smell of the cupboard. Above her the ceiling was squares of natural wood. In places a stain loomed darkly against insipid graining. A raw light bulb hung down above her, a switch at its base. Dust clung thickly to the cotton covering of the wire. Half way up a shrivelled insect, long dead, hung by a strand, swinging gently in the movement of the air. She could see each dried leg clearly, drawn rigidly up against its segmented abdomen. Sun shone warmly through the window on to her face. She could see sky and the soft wavy line of hills. Woven in among dark conifers was the bright cerise of mountain azalea. She felt peaceful looking at the small square view. In the midst of strangeness the mountains remained consistent and familiar, facing or backing everything in Japan.

It did not seem possible only that morning she had been at home. Time had stretched. Home swung distant and grey, far behind her, another dimension. It could have been days since she left. She thought about it then, seeking the comfort of its familiarity. But she found in her mind only a dark house, filled with strange sensations and feelings she did not understand. The sound of her mother's sobbing, the bleak window of rolling cloud, Hiroko's jerking body behind the yellow dress. Hiroko. The house vacant of her mother, and that gap tunnelling through the feelings of each day, making each hour hollow and treacherous. Hiroko. The small soft noises in her father's room. Hiroko. Hiroko. Hiroko. She swelled up larger and larger, looming over each day, every moment threatened by her. Natsuko felt entirely alone. Wherever she looked for help she came back only to herself. Now, on the quilts in the farmhouse, the knots pulled tighter in her head. Turning on her side she clasped her arms about her knees, suddenly cold and shivery. Shutting her eyes she fell into a fitful sleep.

She dreamed she was walking up from the river again, turning off the road at Hiroko's home. Stopping a moment in the yard before the farmhouse she remembered seeing clearly before the dilapidation of the wood and clay walls, the white paper squares of the windows and door, the slope of prickly roof. But now, although the roof was still thatch, beneath it the house had turned to black polished iron. Instead of doors and windows there were eyes and a mouth. She saw with horror the house was a huge head of armour, rising out of the ground. The door had iron teeth about the inner rim, and above a long drooping eave of thatch, like a moustache.

People were going in and out. She tried to hold back but something was making her walk to the door. Stepping over the threshold she was careful to pull her feet up high, so they did not touch the teeth.

It was dark inside. From above a faint light filtered down. Looking up she saw the massive empty space beneath the roof, criss-crossed by layer upon layer of beams, like a jungle gym. The light came from a smoke hole in the roof. She could even see a patch of moving cloud through it. From the left she dreamed she heard Hiroko's voice, calling. Standing in the doorway of the raised, matted living space, Hiroko was beckoning. Natsuko left her shoes and stepped up. Still smiling Hiroko continued to beckon her forward. And Natsuko saw then the room was full of people, all pointing accusingly at her. Their bodies massed together in the small room, sombre and close, deep shadows around their feet. They began to move in about her, silently. Then, from the back of the room, the man in the maroon sweater, Shojiro, stepped forward, coming to get her. He was pulling the white towel from his neck. It kept on coming without end, and she saw it was really a long white rope. Without their speaking she knew their thoughts. They were going to boil her in the vat of shrubs. There was only one chance to get away. She must reach the open smoke vent. Running from the room she gave a tremendous leap, managing to clutch the lowest beam, and swing herself up. She began to climb but was hampered by a thick residue of soot on the beams. It blew up in clouds, filling her mouth, making her throat thick and dry. Once she looked down and saw all their upturned faces. She saw also the curved wall of the hearth was no longer in disuse, but alight. Sunk into its broad counter top, all the rice pots were bubbling and boiling away. The steam chased up after her, winding damply about her hands and legs. But she was nearly there now. She could see the tops of the trees and the sky through the hole of the smoke vent. A soft breeze blew in touching her cheek, and the hair behind her ear. Over and over again she felt it rub across her face . . .

She woke with a jerk, feeling again the soft touch on her cheek, and opened her eyes.

First she saw only the hand near her face, the broken nails and dirt-ingrained fingers. They touched her cheek like rough paper then, gently, the hair behind her ear. From the open palm was a smell of wood. Turning her eyes she saw the ribbed waist of a maroon sweater.

A scream collected in the back of her throat. She remembered where she was, and sat up. At once he was very close, his face directly before her. Terrified, she pushed back against the wall. But, squatting still beside the quilts, he did not move. The canvas socks were gone, bare ankles and feet stuck out of the tight leg of his trouser. They were pale and soft, from the knuckle of each big toe long sparse hairs stood up. He wore traditional worker's trousers, close fitting to the knee, swelling out from there like riding breeches, in a great curved seam. As he squatted the trouser pulled in long taut folds the length of his thigh. The crotch gaped unevenly, a button missing. His hands hung limply over his crouched knees. And still he did not move.

Light in the room was dimmer than before. Dusk was coming on. She did not know how long she had slept, how long he had squatted there, touching her, looking. He smiled, eyes screwing up even smaller behind his cheeks. Pointing to Natsuko's hair he made odd grunting noises, swaying slightly on his haunches. The rough sanded wall grazed her elbow, harsh and cold on her arm. She bit hard on her lower lip, so that the sob should not spill out. Suddenly then, he opened his mouth, pointing inside with a finger, shaking his head.

She understood then. He could not speak, he had no tongue. Terror came up into her dry throat, breaking out between her lips. She could see the stub, there in his mouth. The shock was cold in the base of her stomach, the impact careering about inside her. But her eyes could not stop looking at it, near the dark circle of his throat. It moved up and down as he pointed and grunted, wet and purple, fleshy as raw meat.

Pushing his hands down on his knees, he began to stand up, uncurling slowly. In her ears she heard the churning of blood. This was the moment to run, before he straightened, before he came nearer. Scrambling up she darted forward, pushing into him, knocking hard against the paper door. Her hand flung out, touching a firmness that immediately gave way. She ran across the room to the stair shaft.

Afterwards she could not remember how she got down. Her memory was of dropping the last few steps on to the concrete floor. Only then did she remember her shoes, side by side at the top of the ladder before the matting. Beside them were the limp canvas socks, worn rubber soles upturned to the room, mud caked between the ridges.

There was no time to go back for the shoes. She rushed on out of the workshop, straight into the hard wall of Hiroko. It knocked the breath from them both. Hiroko staggered back, Natsuko panted in short gasps, the collision reverberating in her chest.

'What are you doing? I told you to stay up there.' Hiroko was angry, filled still with shock.

'He's up there. He's up there.' She pointed behind her. It

was difficult to get the words up and out. Each had to be forced separately into her mouth, and transferred to her voice. It was impossible to communicate the fear or revulsion.

'Who? Where? You never can do anything you are told, can you? Stay here,' Hiroko said fiercely, striding into the workshop. There was the drag of her wooden clogs on the cement, and the creak of the ladder. Within a moment she was down, her face set.

'It's only Shojiro. What's the matter with you? He wouldn't hurt anyone. He just wanted to be friends. Now you've upset him.'

'He kept touching me. And he has no tongue.'

'He has never seen hair that colour before. He wouldn't harm you. And think yourself lucky *you* were given a tongue.' Hiroko stepped forward and gripped Natsuko's arm hard.

'Don't try and divert my attention. You hoped I wouldn't notice, didn't you? I thought you were quiet. But you were just sitting there, digging your fingers through the paper doors. Have you seen the hole?' She began dragging Natsuko forward. 'Do you know how much it costs to mend? And they have just been redone.'

'I didn't do anything. I was asleep.' But Hiroko took no notice. Natsuko remembered then as she fell against the paper doors, the firmness that gave way to her hand. It was useless to protest. Nothing would pacify Hiroko, once she was into the rhythm of a mood.

Pulled along behind Hiroko, it was her feet that hurt the most. The sharp points of stones pushed into her shoeless soles. Hiroko did not stop until she reached a clay-walled outhouse, the other end of the thatched house. Here she opened a door and pushed Natsuko in.

'You can stay there until the bath is heated and dinner is

ready. You can get up to no mischief in there.'

The light was suddenly shut away. A lock fell into place outside. For a few moments she beat her palm against the door. A thin strip of light rimmed the bottom near her feet. Bars of shadow moved within it, hesitated, disappeared. She listened to Hiroko's footsteps die away. There was the scrape of the house door sliding open, then shutting.

There was nothing she could do but wait. It would not be long. Until the bath was heated, until dinner was ready. It was already dusk. It could not be for long. She would not cry. That was what Hiroko wanted. She could sit and wait, calmly.

It was not quite dark in the room. It was difficult to make out what it was used for. The floor was earthen, not cemented like the workshop. High up at one end was a narrow, slot of window, thick with dust, half hidden behind assorted oddments. A weak light filtered down from it. Natsuko tried to define the things around her. There was a sour musty smell of earth and wet sacking. Her feet were cold, sore and bruised, but her eyes were accustomed to the darkness now. She made out the large solid form of a box and sat down upon it. The outer corners of the room were in blackness, but under the window light opened up a pile of baskets, showing clearly the wide loose plaiting, the pattern of holes. Garden shears, coils of wire, sticks of wood, protruded here and there. Light touched them wilfully, leaving curious, suspicious shapes and deeper corners. It was stale and dark and unknown. Her heart beat fast in panic, she tried to control herself.

It is all right. It is not dark. She repeated the words to herself aloud. But her voice was that of a stranger, and frightened her further. She clasped her hands tightly on her lap. What if Hiroko decided to leave her here until it was time to go home, the day after tomorrow? No one would know. Her father and Riichi were far away in Tokyo.

She thought of them then, walking round the exhibition. A large echoing stone-floored room, reverberating their footsteps to a high domed ceiling. Their faces bent above long glassed table cases, side by side, interested and serious as they examined small drawings of warriors and court life and battles on ribbons of *emaki* scrolls. Her father would be happy at Riichi's interest. Riichi flattered by his new sense of belonging. Day by day they were both now merging in Natsuko's mind, into one heavy lump, and that often lost behind a mist. Sometimes Riichi still loomed up clearly before her, making her throat contract, but she knew now he was gone. She was alone.

Slowly then the thoughts began to stir in her, turning, gathering speed, round and round inside her head. Anything could happen to her here. Nobody would find her until it was too late. It was like a dungeon. Some people were forced to spend their lives in places like this, treated as animals. She knew about it. For not long before Riichi had told her of a case in the newspaper, he had read it out to Natsuko, line by line. About a man who kept his son in the garden shed, chained to a post, for six years. And nobody knew he was there. The picture in the paper showed the boy, all bent and ragged, blinking at the light. It had upset her for nights.

Everything crumbled in her then. Hysteria worked up like vomit to her throat. The dimness wove about in front of her, the dark solid outlines of shapes dissolving, re-forming, dissolving again. She pressed her hand over her eyes. When she took it away the darkness was full of little dots, pricks of red and silver, swirling and spiralling about her. She gave a sob, retching in fright. Running to the door she screamed and kicked against it, shouting Hiroko's name. Silence. In the thin crack of light on the floor no shadow moved.

She tried to collect herself again. Perhaps if she could reach the window and break it, she might squeeze through, if she manoeuvred her shoulders, if she kept her body flat. Crossing the few feet of space she began to climb, awkwardly, over the dark piled mass of things. Sometimes her feet made a solid find, other times they pushed down deep among hard objects that scratched her bare feet and ankles. The window was nearer, she could see through it the top of the corrugated iron fence outside. An area of light spilt on to her bare arms, then it all gave way beneath her. She fell, rolling over on to the ground, the sacks, baskets, and unidentifiable objects spilling about her.

Sobbing hard, no longer caring, she groped her way to the crack of light beneath the door. Something hard knocked against her hip, her hand came down upon a cold, damp surface. She ran against the door, thumping and crying. Oh God, she thought. Please God let me out.

A shadow moved in the crack of light on the floor. Then the noise of the bolt. She stumbled out into evening light and sweet fresh air.

It did not matter to her now, that it was Shojiro who had let her out. It was only Hiroko she could not have faced. Wiping her eyes on the back of her hand, she tasted salty tears and thin mucous blubbed down from her nose. He was standing in front of her, his slow face screwed up and anxious. In his hand he held her shoes, he put them down before her. Then pulling the towel from his neck, he offered that to her also. For a moment she remembered the dream, how the towel had kept coming and coming, turning to rope. It was damp in her hand now, and warm still from his neck. She dabbed at her face. The towel smelled strong and stale, quickly she gave it back. Silently then he took her arm, and guided her towards the main house.

She knew he was still outside, she could hear small grunts and the peculiar drag of his feet, as he pushed more bamboo logs into the small furnace beneath the bath. Hiroko had said nothing when Shojiro took Natsuko back into the house except, 'The bath is ready'. And that too with her back to Natsuko, washing Chinese cabbages in the sink. She did not speak either as she led the way, crossing from a back door to a small, separate outhouse. Low in the wall, near the ground, was an open hole of fierce colour. Fire burnt deep inside beneath the bath. Following behind them, Shojiro went up to a pile of bamboo logs, green and hollow, stacked against the wall. He began picking over the logs, pushing them into the fire, stoking up the furnace. Beside him the long, metal flue of the bath house breathed black smoke.

Inside it was steamy and warm. The wooden-lined metal tub, sunk square and deep in the floor above the fire, filled with hot water, smoked a damp wet cloud. Hiroko leaned across the bath, and slid open half of a small window. Immediately cool air and black smoke blew in. She made Natsuko strip and wash down on the tiles outside the bath, before getting in. Then, leaving her to soak, she returned to the kitchen.

It was very hot. Sitting on the wooden seat in the bath, the deep water up about her chin wrapped around her like a blanket, comforting. She wished she could just sit here, enjoying the warmth, and relax. But her body and mind remained tense to the sounds of Shojiro outside. And she did not like the dense black smoke, puffing in at intervals when the breeze blew back upon itself, nor the soggy wooden tub. In one corner a soft fringe of splinters waved gently in the water, like weeds. Every so often smoke caught in her throat, making her cough, and then her head throbbed painfully again. She stood up, wanting to shut the window, but beneath it the floor of the bath was right over the fire, and scorching hot. She jumped back, her feet sore from the heat. Standing on the seat she tried leaning across to the window, but was not tall enough. The effort of straining made her head dizzy and she sat back on the seat again. For a moment everything went black about her. She knew she should get out, that she had had enough of the heat. But she still heard Shojiro, pushing wood into the furnace, banking it up so that the water in the tub would stay hot enough for everyone in the house. One by one they would all come here, to wash and soak. Natsuko was relieved she was first. She could not have sat like this knowing Shojiro had used the water before her. Not wanting then to leave its warm protection she waited, until the sounds outside stopped. For several moments there was silence. Standing then, she climbed out of the bath, reaching for the narrow strip of towel Hiroko had left. Folding it she rubbed it down each limb and over her body. But immediately wet vapour settled on her skin, making it damp again. In the bare cubicle adjoining the bath her pyjamas and cotton *kimono* hung. She pulled the clothes over her head, but they clung in awkward folds to her damp, hot flesh. Through the open bath door smoke and steam swirled out, stuck to the walls of the cubicle and ran in dribbles to the floor. On her body sweat turned clammy in the cooler air. She shut the door and ran quickly back to the house, not looking to see if Shojiro still stood there.

They had drawn back the doors of the small room where the old woman slept, opening it up into the next matted space. A group of people sat around a low table, busy over bowls of buckwheat noodles in soup. Their eyes gathered upon the jerking screen of a colour television. They were watching one of several daily *samurai* adventures. Because of their swashbuckling violence her mother objected to Natsuko watching them. Here nobody minded, they just made room for her at the table. Hiroko silently placed a bowl of noodles in front of Natsuko. On the television a blind swordsman, ragged and blanket wrapped, shuffled along the slope of a hill. Mist swirled eerily. The camera followed his straw sandaled feet, and the tap of his stick. The dark gate of a temple filled the screen in a black frame. At its centre a small open door was a bright peep-hole. A path led away from it, hazy and damp, filled by early morning mist. The blind swordsman tapped his stick, walking into the temple, getting smaller and further away. Mournful music played in the background. The camera moved from his rolling eyes to his stick, tapping amongst dry fallen leaves and the wet cobbles. Then the door of the gate slammed shut. The screen was in blackness. Music screamed out loud and stopped. A mug of overflowing beer suddenly filled the screen, then bright honky tonk music and pictures of people surfing, riding huge waves on the sea. Around the table eyes dropped away from the screen, and settled on Natsuko. The people seemed to know her, although to her their faces were strange. They smiled, talking to her, asking questions. But, sitting so near her at the table, they seemed somehow far away. Their expressions and voices appeared distorted and fixed. The loud noise of slurping rolled around the table. Thick noodles fell in shredded tongues, from mouth after mouth to bowl after bowl. Natsuko stared vacantly, unable to speak or answer questions. Tired of persuasion they left her alone and returned to the television screen. The last image of the commercial faded. The drama started again. Now there was a group of bad monks. They were fat and muscular, with shaven heads. There were rolls of fat over their eyelids, their mouths were loose and cruel. They were counting from a box of gold coins. A candle flickered between them, running flaring shadows up the walls, twisting their faces into fiendish black splinters. The sound of their laughter filled the room, hoarse and devilish, eclipsing the slurping.

A door slid open, Shojiro came in. At the table the only space was opposite Natsuko. He walked over and sat down. Kneeling, Hiroko doled out soup and noodles with a long-handled ladle and chopsticks, from a bright patterned saucepan in the middle of the table. Shojiro kept his back to the television, his shoulder half blocking Natsuko's view. On the screen it was midnight. The fat monks were walking through the deserted town. The camera looked down on their wide straw hats, moving between crowded roofs. The only sound was their wooden clogs, clattering along. Shojiro lowered his head and ate quickly, picking up great bunches of noodles between his chopsticks, shovelling them into his mouth, sucking up noisily. On the screen the camera changed its bird's-eye view of the straw hats and came down beside the monks. Behind them they dragged a decapitated deer. The camera zoomed in on the headless, bloody stump of its neck, its thin stiff legs. Natsuko averted her eyes, her stomach cold. Shojiro bit through a mouthful of noodles. They dropped from his mouth and swung limply over his chopsticks. His small slanted eyes stared directly into her face. She looked back to the screen at once. Now the bad monks were dragging a woman from a small house, there was a child with her, crying. It was still night. Screams filled the darkness. The woman was being beaten, her naked back was slashed and raw. The child wept hysterically. Natsuko looked quickly away again. Still staring at her, Shojiro chewed. On the television a door banged, its paper ripped and flapping. The wind moaned loudly. Through the torn door emerged the blind swordsman. Baddies surrounded him immediately, swords drawn. His eyes rolled and blinked. What appeared to be his stick was now revealed as a secret sword. He slashed and cut, bodies dropped before him. Flesh sliced easily. He thrust his sword into a bad monk's stomach, twisting it. The monk vomited blood. Looking quickly away Natsuko met Shojiro's eyes again. He smiled. In his eyes was intimacy, as if they had shared things together. Upon the television slashed bodies writhed. In the space behind, Hiroko's mother groaned softly from time to time. In Natsuko's mind everything was suddenly jerky and strident. The music, the moaning and the slurping slid about in her ears, tunnelling into her head, unbearable. She stood up quickly, and went over to Hiroko.

'I'm tired. I want to go to bed,' she said in a rush.

On the television the music was crashing about, the blind swordsman was getting ready to stab again.

'Well, go up to bed then,' said Hiroko, not taking her eyes from the screen.

Natsuko slid open the main door of the house. Outside it was dark and silent. She knew she must not look anywhere, just keep her eyes on her feet, and walk quickly. She wished she could have asked for someone to come with her. Not looking at the dark clumps of trees or the prickly silhouette of the thatch she walked towards the workshop. She was free of the room behind, of Shojiro's eyes, of the television, and the strange contorted faces about her. But she did not want to go to sleep, because of the dreams, because of all the thoughts and fears knotted up tighter and tighter in her head.

A large moth fluttered outside, against the netting of the open window. Its fanning shape, drumming softly was the first thing she saw as she woke. She was covered in sweat. There had been a hole in the ground, like a deep grave, and she was imprisoned in it, unable to get out. She put her hands over her face, touching, assuring herself of her own reality. The room was not dark, there was a moon. Through the window she saw the soft white drift of clouds across it. Crickets purred above the constant croak of bullfrogs. It was a warm night, and at first she was conscious of Summer night sounds, of insects and frogs. In the moonlight the white quilts and the paper doors of the cupboard and divider glowed bluish grey. The dead insect still swung gently from the wire, the dry segmentations of its body ridged in highlight. Only the first waking moment had been filled by the nightmare. Then, quickly, as always, the thoughts and realities crowded in, one after another. She snatched just a fragment of each before the next rolled down. In the end all the hurts and fears were there and the inside of her mind was like a cloud of wood-shavings, blown up by a gust of wind. All the little bits danced about, knocking into each other, refusing to settle. Sometimes it felt her head would burst. Waking more fully she became aware again of the headache, and a terrible dryness in her throat. Sitting up then she saw Hiroko's bed empty, the quilts thrown back.

From the other half of the room, behind the divider, came a soft sound. It was an animal nuzzling, an intake of breath, a blunted movement. She held herself tense, prepared. Turning she saw first only the dividing paper door, drawn shut beside her quilts. Then, stencilled unevenly across the bottom, a lumpy shadow moved. An arm freed itself for a moment, then fell, lost again in the dark bank of shadow. It was Shojiro, asleep. She remembered when she came to bed, seeing his quilts laid neatly out near the stair shaft. Because of him they had divided the room, drawing the doors closed between them. Lying in bed Natsuko had waited, knowing he must come, determined to stay awake and alert the whole night. Unintentionally she had slept.

The shadow moved again, fluidly, slipping away beneath the bottom of the door, swelling up to fill it again. A large chunk tore free. Briefly the shape of two heads formed.

She pulled back until she was against the rough sanded wall, the cold scratchiness of it rubbing her shoulder. Kneeling cautiously up to the paper door she looked through the hole, torn that afternoon, into the other half of the room.

She had known Hiroko would be there. It crossed her mind briefly what to do if Hiroko needed help. She was unsure of the harm Shojiro might do. But she remembered again the small curranty eyes, and knew anything was possible.

In the other side of the room moonlight was dim and indirect. Washing Hiroko had pinned out in the evening shrouded the window in pale luminous patches, hanging limp and still. There was no breeze. Then she saw Hiroko, the blue splodged pattern of her nightdress. She lay quite still, no sound or movement, as if she was dead. Natsuko felt fearful she was already so. Then, something stirred. Shojiro pulled himself up on an elbow and leaned over Hiroko. Natsuko saw then the buttons of Hiroko's nightdress were open wide. From the window faint blue light spilt on to the slit of her bare flesh. Slowly Shojiro's head came down. He placed his thick open lips against her mouth. His hand crept over Hiroko and disappeared, within the naked gape of the nightdress. The arm appeared cut off at the wrist, the hand plunged deep within Hiroko's body. Her arms lifted up and folded about him. For a moment Natsuko watched their bodies moving and squirming against each other. Then she drew back.

She sat quite still, her back against the cold, rough wall. Her heart thumped, unable to take it in. She had been prepared for every terror but this. Her mind was filled by only one picture. That of Shojiro's open mouth coming down upon Hiroko's lips, fixing there like a thirsty, sucking animal. Nausea and fear rolled up in her. It shocked her most that Hiroko could, without protest, allow Shojiro's freakish mouth to rub upon her own. It was more than Natsuko could absorb, her mind bulged with the thought. Shivering began again in her, gripping her from inside like a giant hand, shaking the bones from her flesh. Her teeth chattered against each other. She turned on her side between the quilts, pulling her knees up, holding herself in a tight ball. After some time the shivering lessened, coming in odd spasmic shudders.

Later the door slid open along the side of her quilt. Hiroko came in, stepping carefully over Natsuko. Slipping into bed she sighed loudly and fell asleep. But beside her Natsuko lay awake, looking at the curve of her back.

[9]

An early morning mist wreathed the mountains. A grey kitten ran across the yard, a power saw whined over the paddy fields from the village. The bushes were festooned with spider webs. It was impossible to ignore the fine clear feeling of the morning. Coming out of the door of the workshop she had seen the bush, and behind Hiroko stopped. It was nearly as tall as Natsuko's shoulder, of tiny, densely packed leaves, covered with the chiffon of cobwebs. Caught within these was the dew, the bush shimmered like rhinestones, reflective and gleaming. Bending close Natsuko looked down and saw each drop of water like mercury, trembling upon the webs. Deeper within the leaves were small black spiders and the bodies of flies marooned in gauze. Discarded beyond the nets was the dry, hollow thorax of a large brown moth. In the pond came a splash of water from the quick tail movement of a fish. Sun swept down over the thatch, in the yard shadows were short and clear. In the middle of this brilliance night seemed a dream, filling another dimension. She was tempted to doubt it had ever been.

But then they went into the dark earthen-floored cavern of the main house. Looking up again she saw the rafters, solid and huge under the massive roof, crossing and recrossing. The feeling of her dreams blew through her again, and fear pricked for a moment in her.

Soon after breakfast an ambulance came, sleek, glossy and ill-fitting in the yard before the thatch. It took the old woman away. Slack and moaning they heaved her on to a stretcher and carried her out. Huddled in blankets there was nothing to see but the thin grey hair of her head, flattened and rubbed away, the pale skin of the scalp showing through. Hiroko's sister-in-law climbed into the ambulance with the old woman. After it drove away the yard seemed suddenly incomplete. Immediately Hiroko drew back all the heavy shutters in the house. Whole walls opened up filling the house with air and light, driving out darkness and stale smells. Hiroko gave Natsuko a bucket of disinfectant water, and together they washed the matting. Hiroko swished up the quilts, stripping them of their white covers, heaving them over bamboo poles outside to air. Soon the house smelt sweet and astringent. In the brighter light Natsuko saw the uneven sag of the large cross beams under the roof, the smooth facets of chiselling along the grain.

Hiroko spoke little. Her hands were wet and red, busy in dusting and shaking, or down on all fours, washing and wiping, her hips stuck up in the air. Soon Natsuko was tired, her back ached, her fingers were all wrinkled and shrunken from the water, her knees full of plaited indentations from the matting. At midday Hiroko stopped, and in the kitchen took from a shelf a plastic cup of instant dried noodles. On to these she poured boiling water and left them to soften. She handed them to Natsuko with an apple, and half a bag of rice crackers glazed with soya sauce and crumbled seaweed. Natsuko took it all outside. Sitting on a stone by the pond, amongst the potted shrubs, she ate hungrily, drawing up the thin noodles from the hot soup, blowing to cool them, before pushing them into her mouth with the chopsticks.

Munching the apple she walked back to the bush she had seen in the morning. Only a few drops of dew still trembled in the webs. The spiders crawled about the surface, busy at the bodies of ants. The nets were dry, the bush looked tired and dusty. In the back of the workshop she could hear Shojiro. Not wanting to go in she walked along a narrow flagged path, round the side of the workshop, curious where it led. It came to a blank stop in front of a wall and two small cryptomeria trees.

Turning back she saw him then, staring at her through a window. He welled up before her, unexpected, like something in her nightmares. The glass of the window was thick and dusty, through it his face unclear, as if behind a curtain, mottled by watermarks and smears. He was smiling, the blackened teeth slit his face. Then he was gone. She hurried quickly away, but the soft dragging sound of his canvas socks came round the corner of the building to meet her. And he was there in front of her, grunting and beckoning.

The night was before her again. Her mind cut off, her feet followed him numbly. The stones of the path were large and uneven, jutting up in thick wedges, green and mossy. Once her foot slipped awkwardly, but Shojiro in his dark cloven socks, trod with the ease of an animal. He turned to grin at her. And having faced him, having seen again his shape and feel, her dread lessened slightly. She wondered if the night had not really been part of a bad dream. For in the sunlight everything seemed without menace. In front of her the canvas socks, the soft pull of sweater on his shoulders, the straight, thick spikes of hair lying close to his head, seemed harmless. In her mind the night receded to a black frozen feeling, that seemed in this sunny yard to hold no reality. The sun on the thatch, the cobwebby bush, the still grey pond before her were all clear and exact in outline. Daylight presented things as they were. It played no deceiving tricks. She was relieved by this temporary reprieve. For a while there was nothing more than what she could see.

The backroom of the workshop was smaller than the front. The window through which Shojiro had loomed was over a low tank of murky liquid. Before it at floor level, a shallow, basin-like seat was hollowed out of the cement. It was filled by a paper cushion, still holding the indentation of Shojiro's buttocks. Between the tank and the seat a deep shaft opened into the floor. Shojiro sat down on the cushion and swung his legs into it. Now at floor level he sat right up against the tank. Dipping his hands into the cloudy liquid he pulled out a wooden frame with muslin stretched across it. Light glowed through it as he brought it out, liquid dribbled down his arms. He balanced the frame across the tank and took up a long-handled metal scoop, holding it out to Natsuko. As she took it he pointed to a bath of thick liquid beside the tank.

The handle of the scoop was wet and chalky where Shojiro had gripped it, and warm still from his hand. She dipped the scoop in the bath and stirred, pushing down deep, then bringing it up to the surface. The mixture was thick as porridge, and the colour of dirty sand. As she stirred the thin, milky top disappeared and a lumpy substance oozed up from below, spilling over the sides of the scoop. It smelled sour as vomit. Shojiro pointed to the baskets of shrub and rock in the next room, to the vat, still simmering gently, indicating it was all in the bath and tank. What she stirred was liquid paper. Curious, she filled the scoop several times as Shojiro directed, emptying it into the bank before him. Then, motioning her to stop, he beckoned her forward.

She did not like standing so near him. Sitting as he did, his head came only to her waist. He appeared a legless midget, his limbs lost beneath the floor in the cramped shaft.

Looking down upon him she saw the soft flesh inside the collar of his sweater, a thick vein at the base of his neck. Around his chin bristles were stubbly as the thatch. He turned, twisting round at the waist, reaching out to a packet of cigarettes and matches beside the cushion. The red wool of his arm touched her leg. Cupping the match in his hand he lit the cigarette. His lower lip pushed out supporting it, showing the wet pink inner skin. The night passed through her like a shadow. Then again it was gone. He turned back to the tank, smiling and grunting for her to watch. Propping the cigarette up in an empty tin, a bright label of mackerel about it still, he picked up the wooden frame and plunged it into the liquid. Shaking backwards and forwards he scooped it up and plunged it back several times. Finally he lifted it out, and she saw a fine glutinous layer, clinging to the muslin. Draining it quickly he stood the frame against the tank, and from beside him removed a bamboo mat from a pile of raw, wet paper. It reminded Natsuko of a cake of bean curd, or the grey top of the camembert cheese her mother sometimes brought. Its surface held the indentation of the bamboo mat. Shojiro tipped the new layer of paper flatly from the frame on to the pile and covered it up again.

Forgetting her fear she watched him add several new layers in this manner, fascinated at the sudden materialization from this murky liquid of raw paper. Shojiro was quick and skilful, scooping and shaking deftly. When he looked at her his eyes were bright and friendly, she allowed herself once to smile. Then abruptly he stopped, scrambled up from his seat, and taking her arm guided her outside. But uneasy again at his touch, she pulled herself free and followed at a distance.

He stopped outside the shed Hiroko had locked Natsuko in the evening before. Now the doors were open wide, light flooded inside. It did not seem the same place. From a distance she saw baskets and sacking, the coils of rope, the box she had sat on, the dusty window. She saw other things too, a bicycle, tins of chemical, an old gas fire, and stacks of wide, greenish wooden planks. She saw also piles of raw paper, lying upon low trestle tables, and remembered the damp flat area she had touched. Beside the outbuilding was another yard, and here the long green planks stood vertically against supports. On them sheets of damp paper were spread, whitening and drying in the sun.

She followed Shojiro into the big outhouse. The baskets and piled oddments surrounded her again. Shojiro was bending over the stacks of wet paper. She stood beside him and watched. From one corner of the pile he rolled up a single edge of paper between the ball of this thumb and a finger. Slowly, carefully, he peeled it all the way back. A thin layer, limp as damp muslin came away in his hand. Gently, he smoothed this on to the wooden board, pulling out the wrinkles skilfully. On the fragile paper his thick hands were pink and soft from the tank. After finishing several boards he began to take them, one by one, outside into the yard.

She heard him stacking them in place, the noise of the wood dragging on the gravel. Bending over a pile of damp paper she touched it gently. It was cold. She peeled back a corner with her nail. The edge was fuzzy as blotting paper, and came away in little soft slubs when she rubbed it between her fingers. She tried pulling as Shojiro had done, but instead of rolling easily off a thick narrow strip, several layers deep, tore off the length of the block. It hung damply from her fingers in a ribbon. Across the surface of the pile was a deep step, its edge lined by the many thin stratas of paper. She stared at it in horror.

The light cut out abruptly. Looking up she saw him there, the door swinging nearly shut behind him, anger in his face. He strode to where she stood, the strip of paper still hanging from her fingers. It was again dark in the room. The narrow gap between the two doors let in a long shaft of light.

She wanted to move, and kept pushing out in her mind with her legs. They did not obey, but stood quite still beneath her. Gesturing and grunting his babbled language, he took her roughly by the shoulders, and began to shake her.

The dark rattled up and down around her. Bright patches of light darted out then sprang back. The beam from the door swung around like a searchlight. Shapes toppled about. Inside her skin the bones jiggled loosely about, her neckbone felt it might soon crack. And all the time, consistent above her was Shojiro's face. Solid, filled with the black holes of nostrils and eyes and mouth, it grew nearer and nearer. His gobbled words spewed over her in a rush of warm, sour breath. Then, suddenly, his anger finished. He stopped, letting go of Natsuko's shoulders. Her knees trembled, her legs were soft and useless, collapsing quickly beneath her.

It all burst within her then. The tight knot of fear exploded, splintering up into her head, down into her legs. Around her pictures of the night careered, of the mouth coming down, fixing upon Hiroko. With just the thought a heat shot through her arms and legs, flinging them out in all directions. She jumped up and ran then, quickly, through the door.

Daylight burst in her eyes. Squares of drying paper swung white and tall above her head, glaring painfully into her mind. Turning from them she ran past the old thatched house and workshop, out into the road, down towards the river.

There was no clear idea in her mind of what she should do.

But she could not go back. That was the only thing of importance in her mind. Once she saw him, running, high above her, across the bridge. She crouched even lower behind a bush on the dry river bed. But he did not look down. Then again, his odd grunting noises came from the road along the river. She flattened herself against the stony bank, and prayed he would not see her. Huge, tightly packed stones stretched away above her in a diamond pattern, to meet the white safety guard of the road. For a moment he stood there, a maroon blur, then he turned away. She waited a while behind the bush, but he did not come back. She heard nothing more.

The river sloped steeply downwards, the force of its descent broken at its steepest part, into several wide steps, so that the river, when full, was a series of waterfalls. But now the bed was dry, covered thickly by long grassy weeds and bushy shrubs. It looked as if it had never seen water. Only a narrow stream moved sluggishly against the opposite bank, trickling weakly over the steps. Near the bridge, behind Natsuko, was the iron ladder, flat against the wall she had climbed down. It ended several feet above the ground. Jumping the last part, she landed badly, cutting her knee. She dabbed at it with her skirt, but blood ran down inside her sock, drying there, sticky and hard.

Keeping close to the stony wall of the bank, she walked cautiously, watching all the time for Shojiro or Hiroko. When she reached the first of the steps in the river bed she sat, sliding her legs down over it as far as she could before jumping. Her skirt pulled up behind her, something coarse scratched the back of her legs. When she stood up she saw the step was almost to her shoulder, covered by long mossy weed. Where the river trickled narrowly it was silky with slime,

147

sleek and glossy behind the falling water. But where it was dry the weed was grey and furry, scratchy as a loofah. Ants crawled in and out of it, dandelions grew in cracks between. A strong, earthy smell hung in the air. Down here the weeds were high and tangled about her feet, half hiding discarded hardware and garbage. She trod carefully around a patch of broken glass beside a rusted pushchair, and a pile of old tyres. Propped against a tuft of weed was an unbroken pane of glass. Crushed under its weight long-stemmed grasses had yellowed and lay, pressed and flat, each blade unmoving, as if in a painting, stiff and still. A broken pink plastic baby bath stood filled with leaves and dirty rainwater. In it floated a spider, dead and bloated, its legs spread limply like a starfish. Before her the river bed stretched away in steps for a while, then regained its level and wound on between deep wooded hills. Along the stepped section the great stone banks soared up, reminding her of the fortress walls at the castle in Himeji. Perched houses stared straight down into the river, their pale walls flush with the stony bank, blended with it in broad squares and perpendicular lines. On top grey tiled roofs crowded darkly into one another.

In the late afternoon sun everything looked very still, far away and quite removed from Natsuko, as if she walked here in a dream. But then she thought of the farmhouse, the dark rooms, the workshop, the tanks of liquid paper, the bushes of spider webs, and that too was possessed of an unreal quality. She began to feel she moved only in dreams, drifting from one world to another. They stretched out behind her like links in a chain, each cell sealed and separate, connected only by her presence in them. Trying then to remember each event and feeling that dragged so heavily with her always, she felt a

148

rushing in her head, like the noise of swirling water, mounting to a splintered point. Here it blurred and broke off, filling her mind with confusion. She could not remember. Slowly, with difficulty, she forced her mind back, and saw dimly the shapes behind her.

She walked on, weeds knotting about her feet, brushing roughly on her bare legs. She manoeuvred the rest of the steps, then the stony banks were behind her, the river was level, a gentle bend, the banks low grassy mounds. Above the sky was broken with clouds, the weather was changing, a light breeze had sprung up. Behind the constant dull throb in her head and the confused emotions, one thought held firm. She could not go back. Not until tomorrow, not until it was time to go home. Under her skin the nerves were alert, that nobody should see her, nobody should catch her or take her back. Not until tomorrow. High above the setting sun broke through dark clouds, spearing a window of a house, setting it briefly ablaze, shiny and orange, so that for a moment she thought it was fire. Then clouds blew across and it was gone.

When she first saw them she hid quickly behind a bush, watching cautiously. But they were small children, much younger than herself. She did not feel threatened, it was safe to walk on. But passing them they looked up and called to her, friendly and excited, crouched in a circle amongst the weeds. She saw the insect boxes then. They held up the little meshed wire cages, and called her to look.

Crouching there among them, she felt their pleasure and excitement. The faces about her were round and smooth as pebbles, the almond eyes, bright as jet, incised clearly in their faces. They did not stop talking. Words poured from them, the sounds jumping freely in the air around Natsuko, loose and easy. There were no shadows in their faces. They were happy at capturing a large stag beetle.

'Isamu did it . . .'

'. . . and I held open the door . . .'

'. . . and he pushed it in.'

'. . . with a twig.'

'I'm not going near it.'

'It fell over on its back.'

Their voices clattered about her, stretchy as bits of elastic. In the little mesh boxes the shelly backs of beetles moved darkly. They pushed Isamu's box near her face. Small grey crickets jumped about, in their midst the huge solid beetle, armoured and crusty, the enormous antlered mandibles waving before it.

She stayed with them for a time, parting the grasses, looking under stones for insects. Once she found a large green cricket, juicy and bright. They showed her how to catch it, cupping her hands round the stem it sat on, shutting them quickly, one over the other. But in her palm she felt the light tickle, and thought of the body, the muscular thighs jumping against her flesh, and opened her hands, letting it free.

It was darkening all the time about her, difficult any longer to see individual leaves and grasses. Shadows began to clump things together, condensing them to broad outlines. The children gave her some sweets and a few rice crackers in a cellophane bag.

'Goodbye.' Their voices sounded back to her as they climbed the low bank, and waved before turning into a cluster of houses.

Natsuko sat for a long while on a stone, looking at their homes, the white squares of quilts hanging from upstairs windows, airing still. They were small houses, wooden and faced by bark, with deep tiled roofs, and small cramped gardens of short thick trees. She watched the lights, one by one, go on behind the windows and grow brighter, while the outlines of the houses faded into the sky. The quilts were pulled in. A smell of frying and piquant soup drifted to her. Above, the bats were already out, fluttering darkly against the last light, twittering like loose screws in the sky. At last there was nothing left but the night, stamped with the brilliant frames of windows. In them Natsuko saw small figures laying out beds, stirring pans. Once or twice she recognized one of the insect box children. A woman with a baby strapped to her back carried things back and forth across a room, another nursed a crying child. There was a smell of burning everywhere. Outside back doors long metal chimneys smoked in a row from heating baths. Natsuko watched the life of each house run into the next. Children played together, utensils were borrowed, women chatted to each other through kitchen windows over sinks. You could put out a hand from any one of the windows, and touch the house next door. The people in these homes were never alone. Natsuko watched them, envious and fascinated. The sky was now an inky stain. She stood up and walked on then, feeling shuttered, small and totally alone.

Further down the river, while looking for insects with the children, she had seen the pipe flue, a large open circle in the river bank. In the daylight then she noticed the pale interior, large enough to sit inside. It was dry and dusty, with dandelions growing thickly about the rim. She knew it was disused, no water ever flowed from it. But now, in the evening, it gaped blackly. She hesitated a moment before climbing in.

It was not as large as it appeared from outside. As she pulled herself inside a fine dry dust settled between her

fingers and over her knees, powdery and smooth. Sitting sideways her feet rested on the vertical curve, level with her
stomach. Her knees came right up beneath her chin. She
manoeuvred round until she sat lengthways, legs straight out,
feet near the entrance, her head just clear of the top. But this
way there was nothing to lean against, and her back soon tired.
In the end she settled for a twisted posture with her legs stretched out and her shoulders resting against the side of the pipe.

It was quite dark now outside. The sky was full of moonlit
cloud, banked flatly together like a frozen lunar landscape. A
breeze blew down the pipe. Natsuko hugged her bare upper
arms with her hands. In the daylight, from outside, she had
not thought about the dark. The pipe faced not houses, but
the silent wooded hills. All she saw was blackness and, along
the top of the hills, a ragged fringe of trees against the white
cloud. The night began placing things uncomfortably before
her. From the back of the pipe came a damp putrid smell.
When the breeze changed direction, away from the pipe, a
soft rotting wave of it pushed over her. It forced her to think
about the pipe, stretching back behind, empty and hollow.
If she coughed or moved each small sound echoed slightly.
And further back, in the narrow emptiness, strange sounds
sometimes boomed, repeating up and down the pipe.
Thoughts expanded under her skin, pricking her nerves. A
picture came into her mind of being sucked back into the
pipe, deeper and deeper, of seeing the hole in the bank rushing away from her, disappearing as the pipe joined other
pipes, tunnelling beneath the village in a labyrinth of com-
plex tubes. Her body would wedge there, clogging the pipe,
decomposing slowly, washing away bit by bit, until there was
nothing left of her but a few bones to slip easily along, out
into the sea. She had thought in the beginning no further

than the dusty entrance. But suddenly now she felt the same panic as when she swam in deep water and thought of the depth below her. She remembered once on a seaside holiday swimming with Riichi, splashing and laughing, trying to keep up with his thrashing body. Ahead of her he turned and stopped, so that she too slowed down and began paddling water in one spot. She had looked down then and seen the dark shadows of rocks, looming murky and threatening beneath her. Instantly panic filled her. She beat the water hysterically, unable to turn, float or swim. Salty water gushed into her nose and mouth. Riichi pulled her back to shore, but not until she felt ground beneath her did the panic leave.

She moved closer to the entrance of the pipe, and tried not to think of the endless narrow tunnel, burrowing behind her. She did not know what time it was, or how long she had been in the pipe. The thick clouds above had broken up, freeing the moon. Thin pale stratas of cloud drifted across the sky, like yards of flimsy chiffon. The silhouettes of branches and leaves were black and lacy. She did not feel hungry, but lunch seemed long ago. She felt she should eat as a means of conserving her strength. Her head beat painfully now and she was cold. She pulled the bag of rice crackers from her pocket, and the two chewy sweets, wrapped in waxy green paper. Having eaten this neither the coldness in her body nor the ache in her head were any better. Stretching out she lay down, pillowing her head against her arm, and tried to sleep. It was a fitful dozing, each time a black falling off, to rise again to the narrow confines of the pipe. Shivering with cold, she rubbed her hands up and down her arms, feeling the breeze blow up her legs and skirt. In the sleeping and waking she did not know if hours or only minutes passed. Then again blackness sucked her under.

She came to slowly, with the feeling of being pulled back into her body, spiralling up into it from a deep and terrible place. When, slowly, she sat up there was a spinning sensation in her head. It bumped the top of the pile, reminding her harshly where she was. Lying back again, eyes shut, her head revolved unsteadily, round and round, heaving her stomach up into her throat, making her feel sick. She was stiff with cold, shivers rattled down her in spasms. At the end of the pipe her feet and ankles were wet. It was raining. She heard the light patter of water on leaves outside. The sound of the trickling river carried loudly in the night, dogs barked somewhere in the village. A light wind stirred grass, rustling like tissue paper. Moonlight shone directly into the mouth of the pipe. She could see the patent sheen of dandelion leaves, raindrops dripping from their ragged edges. At the end of the pipe a wet band rimmed the lower half, the dust had turned to mud. She pulled her feet in, curling up roundly, trying to get warmer. Her socks were soaking wet, cold on her feet. She wanted to take them off, but the thought stayed in her mind, irritating. Her body would not sit up, nor her hands obey. Her head hurt now if she moved her neck, and she was conscious of a pain in her chest. Each time she tried to breathe it closed up tightly inside her, like a fist. It was easier to take short shallow breaths.

From one end of the pipe cold blew in, from the other dark welled up, pulling constantly at her. Somewhere, from the back, she heard a continuous knocking sound, metallic and hollow. The pipe must surface, and rain splattering upon it echo along. She closed her eyes, and again she was falling, turning head over heels, on and on. When she thought it must end she looked down and saw, still waiting, the black beneath her. As she fell Hiroko's face floated up from the opposite direction, came level with her and drifted on. She saw the white teeth, the pink tip of tongue. Then as she watched, it changed. The tongue was Shojiro's, grotesque and obscene. But, when she looked again the mouth was Hiroko's, mocking, smiling, floating away. From behind her voice trailed back. 'Leave her alone. She'll come back by herself, snivelling and crying. Leave her alone.' Alone. The other words faded, except this. Alone. It fluttered, brushing against her, settling a moment in her head, fluttering up again, falling with her, on and on . . .

First it was a circle of light, shining into her face, dancing on the sides of the pipe. And voices, more than one, talking all at once. They sounded distant and confused. The darkness seeped up around her again. On her chest was a heavy weight. She could hardly breathe, she wondered if she was suffocating. Again the light, on her face, and in her eyes, blinding for a moment. Then it flicked away and she saw behind it faces, crowding into the end of the pipe. And hands, pulling at her legs, pushing beneath her, lifting her up.

Above her suddenly the sky shot out in all directions, as if freed from a small container, breathing wide and free. The rain had stopped, the night was clear. Stars glinted, tiny, like pins in a cushion. Somebody put a cool hand on her forehead, wrapped something warm about her shoulders. The brilliant spheres of torches darted about, showing small patches of faces and limbs. A voice was shouting loudly.

'We've found her. Found her.'

The sobs welled up in her then.

[10]

Light. White and cool, above and around her. It was a high ceiling. She saw now the milky bulb and shade at its centre. There was a feeling of air and space. She did not know where she was. And yet she was sure of some familiarity, sure she had been here before, if only she could remember. She stirred on the bed and became aware of her left arm, unable to move. Looking down she saw bandages, tying it to a wooden splint, and the needle, held down in her arm by sticking plaster. From it clear plastic tubes led to bags of liquid, hanging on a metal stand. Still she was afraid to guess, afraid this too might be a dream.

'Ah. She is awake. And how are you feeling, Natsuko? A little better?' The voice came from beside her.

She saw the long pale face leaning over her, the white veil, the black spectacles. She nodded mutely to the American nun.

'Yes, you certainly look a bit better today. My, but you had us all worried, you know. Now, these nasty drips will be finished in a few hours. I think it would be a good idea if you were to try a little soft food at lunch today.' The nun bent at the end of the bed, turning the crank. Her head bobbed up and down beyond the pyramid of Natsuko's feet. The bed wound up. Slowly Natsuko was raised to an incline. Now she could see the room, the pale walls and curtains, and the white bed, spread out before her like a field of snow. Through the large window was sun and Kobe rooftops.

The nun came forward with a wash cloth, towel and brush. The cloth was cool and refreshing on Natsuko's face, hair was smoothed neatly behind her ears. Then the nun plumped up the pillows, settling Natsuko comfortably back upon them.

'Now, just ring if you need me, child. You should feel much more yourself today. You're well through the crisis now, thank the dear Lord.' She paused at the door and then turned back.

'Do you know, by some blessed coincidence, you are in the same room as your dear mother was. Now doesn't that make you feel better already.' She disappeared with a wave and a smile.

The same room as her mother. Yes. Now she understood the pale antiseptic familiarities. For a moment she saw again her mother's stark face, slipping in and out of the beige dressing-gown, and the putty-coloured curtains. She remembered the loose, lost feeling of her embrace, and the silent tears sliding down her cheeks on to the cloth-wrapped box of biscuits. She remembered the noiselessness of those tears.

A breeze from an open band of window slipped coolly across her face and was gone. She lay, quite still, staring from the window at the spread of roofs, and the wide pale sea of the bay. Between, in a ribbon, ran the docks, the chimneys of steel works and breweries. Beside the hulls of ships stood massive red container cranes, rearing up long necks like prehistoric monsters. The view was familiar, home was not far. It lay to the left behind the hospital, much further up the same slope of hill. She wondered now who had brought her here. If Riichi and her father had returned from Tokyo. Her mind was blank as the sheets tucked about her. When she tried to push into it she came against a soft blurred cushion. Beyond that was a buzzing, like interference on a radio, and her head began to hurt. Half her mind seemed blocked off. She wondered if this was not still a dream. The thoughts tired her, making her head too heavy for her neck. Looking up through the clear bags of liquid, the severe lines of the room wobbled fluidly. In the tubes the mixture dripped like a ticking clock. She closed her eyes too weak to think, and slept again.

She woke with a gentle tugging on her arm. Beside her a nurse was unwinding the bandage, freeing her arm from the drip. The plastic bottles were empty, and without the needle Natsuko flexed her hand, examining the swollen blue bruise over the vein. The nurse smiled brightly, she was a young Japanese girl.

'Feeling better? You've been very ill. Going to eat some lunch?' She wheeled up a high trolley of food and pushed it across the bed, against Natsuko's chest. She tucked a napkin in the front of Natsuko's pyjamas, and lifted up the metal covers from the plates. Natsuko looked at the pale minced chicken and mashed vegetables, and felt not the slightest interest.

'Come along. Just a little will get you well and out of here soon.' The nurse picked up a forkful of chicken and fed it to Natsuko. On her tongue the food was thick and tasteless.

'Did I come yesterday? Who brought me here? What is the matter with me?' She was almost afraid to ask the questions.

'Yesterday? Of course not. No. You've been with us three days. Don't you remember? Maybe not. You've been only semi-conscious. Be a good girl, eat this all up. Look at that strawberry jelly. It was your father who brought you here. You've had pneumonia.'

Three days. She could find them nowhere, detect no clues in her mind. Under her bones was only hard packed emptiness. She took another forkful of chicken, chewing it slowly. After she swallowed, little fibrous bits were left in her mouth. With her tongue she rolled them against her palate. There was something, some feeling they connected with. Pushing out her tongue she rolled a bit off on her finger. It was pale and well beaten, like blotting paper. It all broke in her mind then, cracking the denseness. She saw again the fuzzy slubs of wet paper rubbing between her fingers, the long thick strip tearing away from the block. Shojiro. Hiroko. The feelings came then, pouring in coldly. The pictures she saw were still few and distant. But there were feelings now, churning about, breaking through her in waves. But it was all confused, she could separate no strands, only recognize the heavy mass of nerve. As if she had received back a dreaded acquaintance.

She kept trying through the day. At intervals small splinters of memory poked up in her. Quickly she held on to them, trying to fit them to the jigsaw. At tea-time they made her climb off the high bed and walk to the bathroom, the nurse holding her arm. Her legs were without substance. Sitting there she felt faint. Quickly the nurse pushed her head down between her knees. For a moment in front of her eyes it all pricked hotly, pins and needles of flame-coloured dots. Then it cleared, a cool feeling washed through her head. The nurse helped her up, and pressed the flush. With a rushing and gurgling it all disappeared, sucked back into the dark mouth of the pipe, before clear water swelled back into the bowl. She stood quite still then, seeing again, vivid and huge, the dark hollow pipe tunnelling away behind her. She saw the dandelions, bright in the moonlight, rain dripping from their ragged leaves. Then the torches and faces, after that nothing.

He was alone. He came exactly at six, in a lightweight

beige suit, carrying a cellophane box of strawberries. His expression was stern, though he tried hard to smile when he saw Natsuko lying back upon the pillows, washed and free of tubes. Beside the bed he hesitated, before putting the strawberries down on the cabinet. She knew suddenly then, her father was nervous. He kissed her and patted her head. As he leaned over a faint tang of aftershave lotion filled her nose. His lips brushed her cheek, dry as a moth.

'Well. This is much better. Now we shall soon have you home.' He started brightly. 'Riichi and Hiroko wanted to come, but we were not sure how well you might be. I phoned this morning, did they tell you? They said you were still very weak.'

Ignoring the chair he sat down on the end of the bed. His weight pulled the sheets tight across Natsuko's toes. He looked smooth and clean. Seeing him, she remembered suddenly the dry knotted hair of the doll in her lap, and from the next room his sharp voice. 'But why? Why must you go to places like that, Frances?' Later she had seen her mother, after the doctor came, lying quietly in bed, exhausted. Tears wet her hair, plastering it flatly about her ears.

'Who brought me here?' she asked him then.

'I did. The doctor insisted you come. You were very ill, you know.' Relief showed plainly in his face, hearing her speak.

'I have been so worried about you.' He leaned forward and took her hand, squeezing it hard. 'Thank God you are safe. I haven't been able to concentrate on anything since this happened. Today I cut my last lecture nearly to half, to rush here as soon as I could.'

A confusion of feeling tightened his throat. The relief of seeing her at last, awake and fully conscious, made him feel quite weak. He reached out with his other hand, clasping her fingers between both his palms, feeling their small unyielding frailty. He patted her wrist with his fingertips. He knew if Frances were here instead of himself, she would throw her arms about Natsuko, nearly drowning the child in her own relief. But for all the years he had lived with Frances he had never learnt this easy demonstrativeness. He looked upon it sometimes with distaste, sometimes with envious trepidation. But now he wished, for a moment, the iron in him might break, that he could do more than just sit here, patting the child's hand, repeating, thank God, thank God.

'I don't remember anything.' Natsuko looked away, not wanting him closer. All she wanted were answers to her questions.

'Hiroko phoned me. We had just got home from Tokyo. I told her to bring you straight back in a taxi.'

'When?' Just hearing the name fall, loud and rounded from his mouth, was enough to bring the physical presence of Hiroko up sharp before her again.

'On Sunday evening.'

She remembered the torches, the people, the sky shooting out in all directions, starry and dark. It had been night when they found her. It had been Saturday. She remembered it all now. That meant a whole day, until the following evening, she had been at the farmhouse with Hiroko. In her mind were stray pictures that fitted nowhere. She had kept brushing them away, thinking them remnants of strange dreams. Now she was not so sure. There was a picture of the old woman's bed, laid out, but empty, with herself being lowered into it. And a terrible fear, as the cool covers touched her, that she would die there, her insides rotting. Insects would come down from the rafters and up through cracks between mats, to feed upon her. Another picture was of trees and sky, upside down, refusing to be righted, moving like a film through a car window. These things were not dreams. She knew now they had happened.

Her father looked up, opened his mouth as if to speak, gave a little cough and looked away again. Then he turned determinedly back to her, smiling too brightly, his eyes a narrow slanted crease. Natsuko saw with surprise they were moist with emotion.

'Well. They will be happy to hear you are so much better. I expect they will come tomorrow to see you.' She could hear the nervous effort, the ill ease in his voice.

'I don't want to see her. I don't want to see Riichi.'

'Natsuko. That is not the right attitude. Hiroko has been very good. With your mother away it is not easy, I know. Hiroko has been so worried about you.' His voice was suddenly full and strong. Through his relief annoyance surged up now. She did not seem to realize how much she had worried them. He was suddenly angry. There was not even a splinter of repentance in her. Her chin was all puckered and hard, her lower lip the usual stubborn pout. He swallowed, trying to control his resentment, patting her hand quickly again.

She thought, I hate you. I hate Riichi. Neither of you care. Aloud she said, 'I hate Hiroko.'

Annoyance and alarm passed over his face. And suddenly then, she felt herself strong.

'I hate her. I hate her,' she said again, screaming it out, watching his face grow red and flustered.

'Now, Natsuko. That is not the way to speak. You are ill, I did not want to talk about it but I have heard of the way you behaved at Hiroko's. And really, I am most ashamed.

Ashamed. We will not say anything more now, you are still too weak. But I do not want this nonsense. Don't think I do not know all that has happened.'

He spoke out firmly and fluently. She knew this was what he had come to say, what he had been waiting three days to tell her. She wished then he would go. Hiroko would have told all kinds of cunning tales. It was useless explaining. He would not believe her. All she wanted now was to be left alone. She felt weary. The sight of him, sitting on the end of the bed, tired her out. Closing her eyes she silently willed him to go away. She wished she could spend her life in this calm, light room, and never go home. Never see any of their faces again.

She found the thought in her then. She allowed herself to think it for the first time, I hate them. Yes. I hate them. The thought was round and solid, filling her up. So that she did not need to look at him. So that she could turn her head to the window, and not hear his questions, nor bother to answer them. And she knew then, the thought would never leave her. It would be with her always, holding her up, making her strong. She could depend upon it always.

'Well then. Perhaps I had better go. I can see you are still very tired. Perhaps tomorrow you will be more yourself, and feel like talking.' He stood up at last, kissed her again and left.

The door clicked shut. Opening her eyes immediately, she resettled herself purposefully in the bed, to think more comfortably. She poured the thought through her again and again, examining it, feeling it build up, hard as iron. I hate them. I hate them. And suddenly she felt as if a door were shut behind her, closed for ever. Nothing and nobody could ever hurt her again. Just now, in these few moments, the change had taken place. She was no longer the same person. The old, shivering Natsuko was gone. Now she could do whatever she wanted. Each moment was there to do as she wished with, each situation was hers to manoeuvre. She felt she had made a great discovery, although she could give it neither form nor name. Exhilaration made her suddenly more tired than any physical weakness. Excitement thumped through her skull. She would never need any of them, ever again. She turned on her side then, cheek against the cool pillow, and smiled. Closing her eyes she allowed the thought freedom, feeling it wash deeper and deeper, silently fortifying every cell.

I hate them. I hate them. I hate them . . .

[11]

It was the day of the Summer Festival. From noon the sound
of the drum reiterated down from the small shrine up the hill.
It was hot, the hottest day yet of the Summer. And he was
gone again to Tokyo, for a conference this time, without
Riichi. But it was all right. It did not matter to her any
longer. He had told them the day before, at breakfast, wiping
toast crumbs from his small mouth with a napkin. And she
felt nothing. She had only thought of the things she planned
to do.

Even the brass knob in her hand was warm. The white net
curtains, gathered tautly on wire up against the glass,
smelled hot and dusty. She bent, pulling up the bolts, and
pushed open the french windows. Sun and heat met her
flatly. Stepping down on to the patio, hot concrete burnt
through her bare feet. She ran quickly across it and down on
to the lawn.

Sun glared harshly in the garden, heating colours to a
molten pitch. The greens of leaves and grass ran easily into
one another, acid and lime. The pinks, blues and oranges
of flowers were sharp points or dazzling masses. In the fir
trees cicadas unleashed hysterical whirring screams. She
screwed up her eyes against the sizzling light, and looked
back at the house. Behind the open french windows the
lounge looked cool and secret. Usually in Summer the doors
were wide open, filled by a netted screen. On the patio outside were bright plastic garden chairs and her mother, reading

magazines or writing letters. There were jugs of home-made lemonade, and a huge plastic pool they sometimes inflated and filled with water. Now there were only the shut-up rooms, heat seething and stagnant within them. Summer lay around her like a lake devoid of movement, languid, sun reflecting glassily as far as she could see.

It was this stillness that obsessed her most. It was something she could see and feel, lurking beneath the centre of each long day. Sometimes, in the middle of a room, or half-way up the stairs she would stop, feeling it close in about her, knowing it was there, evil and rotting. And always the feeling of it waiting, for what she did not know. Stillness was there in the hot polished wood of the piano lid, closed and burning beneath a fine dust. It was in the tidy deserted kitchen after the midday meal, and on muddy toned pictures staring vacantly from walls. She saw it on the loquat tree, in rotting unpicked fruit, the soft brown sores crawling with maggots. In the dead of lazy afternoons it inched nearest, breathing gently at her side. It followed her into the heat and lay just below the harsh whirr of cicadas, sucking the sounds into itself. In thick fleshy leaves and the shadow of bushes she saw it move, something decayed, whispering to her over live bodies. It was a sweet stench in the perfume of roses, and the cool soil under stones.

In the morning the walls of her room were white and fresh, and the stillness rested. She could play then as they told her, quietly, lying when tired on her bed. But she could fit the blue sky and the Autumn forest of the jigsaw by heart, the dolls had been dressed and undressed many times, the plasticine models of dinosaurs were sticky to touch in the heat, the books all read several times over. She no longer felt fretful or weak, it was over a month since she left the hospital.

And through the day the stillness grew, crawling and threading its way through her mind. A gossamer-fly. An intangible thing with transparent tracks, it filled her body with restlessness, and left mad thoughts flitting through her mind. It drove her to run wilfully then, to the empty rooms of the house, touching, looking, seeking things she could not see, secrets she did not understand.

Sometimes then, she went into her parents' bedroom, locking the door behind her, and opened the cupboard. From the limp crush of dresses, silently dejected on their hangers, came the smell of her mother's body, reaching out faintly, stirring the air. On a shelf above handbags were stacked, dust in the folds at their sides, and old shoes, carrying the soft bulge of her mother's toes. She pushed her head deep into the cupboard, rubbing the dresses over her face, trying to find limbs and bones, the hard packed body beneath the folds. But she found only cloth, lifeless and empty, imbued with the smell of perfume and sweat. In the drawers scarves, gloves and nylon stockings were no more than piles of rag, only a fine ladder or frayed seam gave them for a moment reality.

At night crickets purred loudly near her window, frogs croaked wetly, piercing her dreams. So that she woke abruptly through splintered fragments of nightmare to hear, always, small sounds in the room next door. The whisper of voices too low to be caught, the soft opening and shutting of doors, the sustained creaks of the bed. Once, she wandered out and saw Hiroko, naked but for an underslip, disappearing quickly downstairs. She heard her father running water in the bathroom. The bedroom door stood open wide. A low lamp diffused the room, lighting the bed to a huge white square. She went in and stood beside it. The covers were all heaped back, half on the floor, the pillows dented and crumpled, a few tight hairs curled upon the empty sheets. Beyond was the window, black with night, the curtains undrawn, the lights of the town like a forest of fireflies. Natsuko's feet touched something rough. Forgotten on the floor beside the bed were Hiroko's beige raffia slippers. She felt ice again in her belly, and the shivering begin in her knees and jaw. Just as it used to before all soft feelings were pumped from her. She ran back to her room, but the shivering persisted. It ripped her apart and left hours of damaging vulnerability, while sleep floated out of reach.

For two days she had watched the gardeners pruning, trimming and cleaning the fir trees. With light ladders and ropes they crawled over the trees like a species of insect, wide straw hats on their heads, scissors at their belts. The trees were inspected, old needles thinned out, young shoots snipped off, and obstinate branches trained along thin bamboo sticks. She waited impatiently for them to finish. At last they were gone. She walked across the lawn to where the hollyhocks grew, towering up against a wall. She had made up her mind, there were two things to be done this afternoon. Crouching down before the hollyhocks, she reached in among the tall stems. Half buried in the soil, right at the back, against the wall, were the toy cups and plates she had used the Summer before, when Riichi still helped her make mud pies. She had mixed mud on the large flat leaves of the hollyhocks. And Riichi brought her water from the garden tap, carrying it carefully in the small red cups. Now she hardly saw him. School had finished. He had a Summer holiday job, working half day in a garage at the bottom of the hill. Even when he was home he spent the hours silently, in his bedroom or the bathroom, behind locked doors.

She pushed the cups aside, except for a broken one which she used as a trowel, digging quickly into the soil. It was dry and firm, she pressed hard and the broken rim of cup pushed uncomfortably into her palm. Once she dug up the soft white bodies of centipede nymphs, their few red legs clustered at one end. Hollyhock leaves brushed her neck and ears. From the shrine up the hill the sound of the huge drum was loud and constant, filling the garden. Somewhere, not far down in the soil, was the metal cough drop box in which she and Riichi had buried the birds. They had found them one Spring, tiny bald fledglings with waxy beaks, fallen from the guttering around the house. Riichi climbed up and discovered the empty nest, and the discarded skin of a snake. He brought it down and made her touch the diaphanous papery tube. Holding her finger he ran it over the transparent scales until she screamed for him to stop. Then they had found the metal box and buried the cold, bald birds.

Green paint and the picture of brown cough drops was still visible on the tin, after she brushed off clinging soil. Her fingernails were clogged with earth. The lid of the tin was closed securely, it took a few moments to pry it off. As it loosened she paused, taking a breath before pushing it up. A bad odour lifted in a slab, then equalized in the air. The little bodies were all shrivelled and brown, like twisted bits of leather. There were no maggots, nothing rooted. Relieved, she looked at them, still able to make out the line of a beak.

She had forgotten about them until a few nights ago. But remembering, the bland contentment of that Summer came back to her. Of her mother stretched out to the sun in a deck-chair, on a table beside her a frosty jug of lemonade, the ice cubes in it smooth and diminished, bobbing at the surface. The sweet sour taste of it filled her mouth while the coldness flowed down into her body. And Riichi, coming across the lawn to her, smiling. In his hands the little red cups of water, his fingers wet and dripping, his knees clinging with earth and bits of grass from kneeling beside her.

And remembering the birds then, she knew at once she did not want them there, peaceful and sealed beneath the soil. They were relative to memories that were now no more than the substance of dreams. Then and there, in the middle of the night, she had wanted to get up and dispose of them.

She carried the cough drop box over to the gate, walking down the steps into the narrow road. The sound of the drum pulsed in her ears, vibrating from the shrine, ricocheting down the hill. Suddenly, cutting through the beat, came the sound of a plane, droning overhead. An amplified voice filled the sky, colliding then transcending the rattling cicadas and drum. It advertised a new supermarket down in the town. The prices of onions and Summer vests echoed resonantly down from the clouds above. The plane circled twice and flew on, the voice trailing fainter and fainter, the cicadas and drum taking precedence again. Looking out over the slope, across the panorama of the town, she saw the new super-market. Floating up on long streamers, from the roof of the yellow building, were six gigantic red balloons. She threw the cough drop box at them, as hard as she could. It came apart against the sky, the birds tipped free and dropped silently into the grass. The box and its lid followed with a rustle. Satisfied, Natsuko turned back to the house.

The kitchen was deserted. A wall of creeper near the window hampered light any time of day, it was always dim. Afternoon silence filled it now, soaking into wood and the empty sink, settling over the wiped surfaces of the table and draining board. The only sound was a hum from the refrigerator, a defrosting trickle somewhere in the back. Upstairs Natsuko had heard the shower in the bathroom, pattering against tiles and the plastic curtain. Hiroko was in there, bathing. Natsuko listened outside, making quite sure before she came down.

The stillness gathered about her now, she felt it crowding behind, watching, waiting. Quietly then, she went into Hiroko's room, closing the door. For a moment she stood, not moving, feeling the room and the smell of Hiroko. Slowly it settled about her, allowing her in.

She began then, touching gently, turning things over, looking, not knowing exactly what it was she must do. But sure it would be shown her. The room was stifling hot. The matted floor held the heat and eased it up to the ceiling. Sweat broke through her tee shirt in wet patches, and collected at the back of her neck beneath her hair. She switched on the standing fan in a corner, and immediately the heat was whipped and beaten. Natsuko looked round the room hesitantly, unsure of where to begin. Then, stepping forward she knelt down before the mirrored cosmetic box on the floor. It was like a small dressing-table, but legless, a stout wooden box with a mirrored stand. She pushed her face up close to the glass, filling it with herself, nose against it, her breath stamping fuzzy patches. There were several bottles and jars on its flat top. Unscrewing them, Natsuko smelled each in turn. Her nose bloated with the thick scents, as she breathed them deep into herself, and blew them out again into the room. Sticking her fingers into the jars of smooth cream, she left long holes in them, and a cool, soft residue on her skin. She rubbed this into her hands until they were moist and shiny and smelled like Hiroko. Pulling out the drawers of the cosmetic box she examined lipsticks, pencils, a nail file and comb, a wrist-watch, a tube of burn cream and a bottle of pills. Slipping off the cap of the lipstick she broke the coral stick at its base, and thrust it back again into the case. Red grease was left all over her fingers. She wiped them on the matted floor. Then she continued, picking up each thing, turning it in her hand, weighing it, pressing her fingers lightly about it. Opening the deep Japanese cupboard in the wall, she pushed her hands between the folded quilts of bedding in the lower half, and on the shelf above fingered a pile of blouses and underwear. Turning back to the room, she saw a blue biscuit tin in a corner of the floor, a green exercise book and pencil rested on top. It was filled with accounts, rows of neat *kanji* characters and figures. With the pencil Natsuko drew fine scribbled lines over each page, breaking the smart columns and the neat little totals. In the biscuit tin were bright spools of thread, scissors, and a red felt cushion shaped like a strawberry, stuck with needles and pins.

Touching each thing Natsuko thought, all this is hers. This is where she sits, this is where she sleeps, these things touch her body, her skin, her nails and hair. And all the time she photographed each thing in her mind, pressing it into herself so that, after she left the room, she would still be there, at the centre of each object. Every secret particle of Hiroko would be diluted by her knowledge of it. Then, at last, there would be nothing Natsuko did not know, no more deceptions, no more secrets. As she went on, touching and thinking, she felt power rise up in her, strong. There is nothing now she can do to me, she thought. I know about her now. I know each secret thing.

Standing by the window she trailed her fingers over the

blue curtains, remembering how she and her mother had hung them there, the day before Hiroko came. The room looked out on to the same creepered wall and washing line as the kitchen. A large laurel bush spread below the window, its pale speckled leaves touching the glass. In the fork of a stem a large praying mantis crouched, looking at her, moving its head as she trailed her fingers across the glass. Its bulbous green eyes never left her, watching, anticipating, front legs drawn up ready to strike. The quality of its gaze disturbed her. She turned quickly from the window and was caught by her own reflection in the mirror of the cosmetic box. In the cheap glass she was all distorted, her body too small, her head too large. In her face the eyes were squashed into a narrow band under the high precipice of her forehead. As she moved the band across her face wobbled and sank, condensing next her nose and mouth, pushing her eyes up high and wide. Behind her a circle of sun glinted on the window, lighting up the room.

She saw then it had all been for nothing, this soft looking and touching. Instead of secrets she knew only the shape and colour of things, only walls and cloth, bits of metal and plastic, a thought, a smell. Nothing. In this room even her reflection was manipulated as she watched, wiping out everything, reducing her to no more than squat features and obedient curves.

Deep in the house she heard the dull bang of a door, and drew a sharp breath, alert. But only Riichi's soft whistling came, and the sound of his feet walking upstairs. It was not Hiroko. Her body relaxed, then filled with anger and frustration. Something hard knocked within her, seeking a chink, a way out. Something. There must be a way to leave a trace of herself upon these things. At once the thought came quickly into her mind. She bent first to the sewing tin, and then from the cupboard took a clean folded blouse from the top of the pile. The scissors were difficult in her hand, a small handleless Japanese shear. She had to bring the two blades together with pressure from the palm of her hand. But soon the cloth began to cut. The soft threads parted before the blades, shredding quickly, even the double cloth of the collar and the frilly edgings of lace gave way. As she cut Natsuko felt strong again. The feeling surged up in her. She thought, there is nothing now I cannot do. For she saw she had only to find the right way. Snip. Snip. The scissors moved quickly in the cloth. A sleeve came away in her hand, the threads all frayed at the edges. Snip. Snip. She understood now. Each strength in Hiroko must be met with an equal strength. From now there could be no half measures, no turning back. She saw it clearly. If she dared, there was always a way.

There was no mistaking the steps now. They came briskly down the stairs, turning, coming along the passage to the kitchen. There was no time to hide the blouse. She left it all there, the scissors and little snipped pieces, in a soft pile on the floor. Running out quickly into the kitchen she ducked under the table. The green checked cloth hung low each side, she saw only Hiroko's bare legs and the beige raffia mules passing by. As the door pushed shut behind Hiroko, Natsuko crawled out, running from the kitchen, behind her she heard Hiroko shout.

There was nowhere else to run to, nowhere else she had thought of to hide. But still, she was surprised to find herself here, surprised nothing but this had registered in her mind. For it was weeks since she had been inside the study. By day she deliberately avoided it, ordered to play quietly by herself or rest. And in the evenings, since she had been ill, she went to bed extra early, no longer required to sit with her father and Riichi. They were as relieved as she.

But now she stood in the study, alone. It was cool, as always in Summer, the windows well guarded by close growing trees. A silent green dimness spread over everything. The room appeared larger than it was, and filled by something solid. She saw the empty space, contained by the walls, floating above the levels of desk, sofa, chairs and books. Yet she was not deceived. She knew, beneath the emptiness, the stillness was packed in tight here. And she was sure then, this was where it generated, oozing out silently, coating the house.

The armoured suits sat just as always, quietly facing her, side by side. Their bodies held those square human shapes that had died or been absorbed in them. She tried to think of the warriors who might once have worn the armour, trudging hills, waving swords and shouting fiercely. But in her mind walked only the empty armour, the bodies inside dissolved, sucked into the iron and lacings. And suddenly she knew, all the stillness bred there, in the very centre of those hollow bodies, flowing out through the holes of their eyes and mouths. She felt it then, coming towards her, entering at the base of her belly, filling her flesh, her mouth and veins, until her body was packed tight as the room, and beat in terror. She stood quite still, unable to move, feeling it claim her entirely.

Upstairs the banging of doors seemed distant. Hiroko's voice screamed her name again and again. Above the study her feet stomped around Natsuko's bedroom, throwing open the cupboards, flushing out each hiding place. Soon she would stamp down here, to the study.

She realized then, there was nowhere really in the room to hide. Only in her mind did it possess such secrecy. In reality each thing in the room was bare of depth or closeted space. The bookcases were glassed, flat up against the walls, beneath the desk space was wide and open to view, the sofa straddled freely the middle of the room. There was only one corner, only one dark hiding place. Behind the low screen of calligraphy, standing at an angle across a corner, right behind the armour.

Putting her hand on the doorknob she turned then, preparing to leave the room, to run. But the footsteps were coming now, down the stairs. They would begin soon up the corridor towards the study. There was nothing now she could do. Nothing. Each way was certain death. Each way the blood within her would stop, and her mind burst into pieces smaller than dust. Letting go of the doorknob she turned back, and walked deeper into the room, closing her eyes, the palms of her hands clammy with sweat.

When she began to breathe again she purposefully took small shallow breaths. Her lungs must not fill too much with the air of this corner. She crouched down behind the screen, as low as she could, head nearly touching her knees, hands still over her eyes. Along the skirting of the wall long settled dust gathered in furry lumps, like mould. Beside her the screen was backed by old temple records, inventories of incense and offerings, yellowed and stained by age. Just once she had looked up and seen the domes of the helmets, knobbled by rows of iron warts, the shoulders hunched and flapped, crusty with metal, hovering darkly above the screen. She was near enough to reach out and touch, near enough to see the plaited texture of the lacing, the frayed chinstraps, the hog-hair moustache, the black iron nose. They loomed above her, dark and cold. She pressed her head to her knees again, unable to do anything but breathe the stale air, filled by the mustiness of ancient things. The stillness here was dry as old bone. She waited, her body contracted and locked, for the end of all things, for her head to crack open in fear or damnation.

Along the skirting the dust moved, lifting slightly as Hiroko flung open the study door. Her footsteps paused, walked into the room, hesitated. Natsuko could see her now, through the slim gap where the screen met the wall. She marched boldly up to the window and swished back first one floor-length curtain and then the other. Turning, she ran her eyes about the room, thinking. She still wore only a brief pink nylon underslip, as she had come down from the bathroom, naked beneath it, too suddenly enraged to pull anything on. Natsuko saw the anger in her, pumping her chest up and down, gleaming hard behind her eyes, settling in a damp line on her upper lip and the moistness of her neck. Through the silky sheen of the petticoat her thighs were hard and tense. Natsuko knew there was nothing, no madness in that fever she would not attempt. She squeezed herself lower, holding her breath, waiting for the moment of discovery, when her mind would completely cease.

Hiroko's eyes settled slowly on the screen, narrowing. Her body turned towards it, then jerked back suddenly. Her eyes stared out in front of her, their expression inquiring, her eyebrows raised. At the other end of the room came the sound of the door shutting, softly. Silence. Natsuko could see Hiroko, standing very still, staring intently in front of her.

'She isn't here. She must have run out,' Riichi said.

'You're home early.' For a moment Hiroko paused.

'What is it? What do you want?' She stood quite still, shoulders drawn back, head tilted to one side, hips up against the sofa back.

Through the crack Natsuko watched Riichi move towards Hiroko, until he stood close to her, only a narrow gap parting their bodies. He was taller than Hiroko, her head came level with his ear as she stood looking up at him, face thrown back. Then something stirred beneath her skin, altering slightly the shape of her eyes and mouth. Slowly, a thick smile formed. And from her lips breath released in a low note of surprise.

Riichi raised his arm then, until his hand hovered above Hiroko's bare shoulder. Natsuko saw the tremble of his fingers as he touched Hiroko's bare flesh. His face turned a little then and Natsuko saw the strangeness, the queer hot glaze to his eyes. She knew his mouth must be dry and his eyes jerk disconnectedly, while words dried flat upon his tongue. Suddenly, roughly, he pushed the thin satin straps off Hiroko's shoulders, pulling the slip to her waist. She stood before him naked. A shudder passed through him. He drew back a little, standing quite still, hands dropped to his side. Natsuko watched a trickle of sweat run behind his ear, through the bristles of his short cropped hair, down his neck, into his collar. Under the thin shirt she saw the movement of his muscles and dark, wet areas of sweat.

The moments stilled about them. She did not know how long they waited, standing there like that, looking at each other. Only the sound of the clock sliced through to the very centre, knocking impatiently in the silence, rattling in and out of her brain.

Then Hiroko began to laugh silently, her mouth spreading open, her shoulders shaking gently. Reaching up she pinched the side of Riichi's face.

'Come then,' she said softly. 'You have much to learn if you want to be your father's son.' She took his face between her hands, and pulled it slowly down towards her.

Natsuko buried her face then, down against her knees, not wanting to look or hear any more. The blood thundered in her ears, swirling in behind her eyes, loud as a waterfall. She wished for the floor to melt and absorb her, she wanted to shrink to the size of an ant, to crawl away, to lie forgotten in the cracks of the skirting. So that she might be blind and safe, so that she might see nothing else. For there was no room now in her mind for anything more. It would burst and split open, like the shell of a nut upon its soft kernel, if forced to a further dimension. About her the room was silent. In her swollen head the ticking clock knocked against her skull, pushing in, pushing out, pushing in, pushing out, drilling small holes in the bone. And faintly, curling in from outside, persistent, hypnotic, came the beat of the drum from the shrine up the hill.

When slowly she raised her head and looked again, the room seemed empty. The sofa back faced her, bare. For a moment she thought they had gone. Her body was soaked in sweat, wet clothes clung tightly to her skin. She sat up and looked again.

First it was the limp, untidy pile of clothing she saw. The soft pink slip, a bit of crumpled nothing, the boards of the floor staring through the empty loops of its satin straps, and the white shirt, its damp patches depleted. Then, mirrored clearly in the glass of the bookcase she saw them, spread upon the wide seat of the couch.

Against the pale green cushions the glass reflected a mound of flesh, an untidy and naked jumble of limbs, rubbing and moving over each other. And through the flat nude sequences of thigh and back broke the vivid titles and binding of books. *Edo Painting, Traditional Domestic Architecture, Jomon Pottery, The Art of the Japanese Screen.* The words pushed forward and receded, dilating and swaying amongst the mass of flesh.

The room was filled with murmured breathing. Natsuko

felt she had woken from a nightmare to the dark again. She felt the stillness had reached out at last, placing its hands about her neck, squeezing until her flesh burst like ripe fruit, draining life from her forever. Every thing kept within her choked up, alive, exploding in her head, slicing through the mangled feelings.

'No. No. No.' She pushed out blindly with her arms, screaming the words.

It all fell about her then, crashing and clattering. She saw it coming down on top of her, wobbling and tippling, parting as it fell. The helmet knocked hard against her ear, the iron warts touching her cheek. The flaps and plates, the clawlike hands and short loose legs fell upon her and rolled away. She felt the weight and scratch as the cold metal heaped upon her skin. The screen lay flattened before her, wide rents opened up in its smooth brushed ink and paper, freeing her to the room. She stood up, pushing everything off her. The evil iron heads rolled across the floor, parting from the helmets. The black masks fell away and lay solitary and diminished. The holes of their eyes and mouths stared blankly up, filled with the pile of a beige rug.

Looking back at the door, she saw their heads and the beginning of their naked shoulders protruding above the back of the sofa, confusion and alarm on their faces. She ran then, holding her hands over her ears.

[12]

Her mother had warned her not to go into tall grass in
Summer, because of snakes. But she was not afraid. There
was nothing she was afraid of now. Her mind was clear. She
knew exactly what she must do. It was the only way. And
afterwards everything would start from a fresh point in time,
there would be no residue to mould the future. It would be
a new beginning. The pictures in her mind would all be
dead.

In the winter once, she had come here, climbing down the
steep drop in front of the house, into the tall yellow pampas
grass. She had seen a snake hole then, a round black opening
tunnelling down into the earth. She had thought of the sluggish, sleeping snakes, coiled deep in the soil, and ran quickly
home. Now it seemed a trivial worry. She knew nothing like
that would ever touch her. A muddy coloured lizard ran
over her foot, a dark oiled stripe down its back. Beside her
ants laboriously scaled long blades of grass, a swarm of
dragon-flies hovered above, sun reflecting on the thin membrane of their wings. The grass reached higher than Natsuko's
head. Twisting among it was a carpet of large leaved con-
volvulus, great spears of golden rod and pampas grass
clumped thickly together. Crouched down deep it was hot
and humid. There was a close, sweet smell around her, alive
with rustles, mites and mosquitoes. Her arms and legs were
all bitten and red, streaked from scratching. Her whole body
itched unbearably.

From the shrine the drum was beating up a final frenzy. Then it stopped abruptly. For a moment the sudden silence was startling. Then, slowly the quietness regained shape, and flowed gently between the clouds and grass. Soon, as they did each year in the Summer Festival, a group of young men would bring out the *mikoshi*, the portable shrine, carrying it high on their shoulders, running with it through the local streets.

From the grass Natsuko kept her eyes fixed upon the house. It stood upright and stiff, exposed to view. Behind the firs and cryptomeria, its expression was obstinate, staring mournfully out at the bay, dark paint on the windows and guttering peeling. She sat for a long time, waiting. A ladybird settled on her hand and walked the length of her arm. Her body was drenched with sweat, inflamed with the constant irritation. But at last Riichi came out, wheeling his bicycle, and disappeared down the hill towards the town. She stood up then, knowing the time had come. Behind her the sky and sea were pale, polished smooth as silver.

Quietly, she went into the house, watching with each step, checking the silence and emptiness. But there was no sign of Hiroko, only stillness everywhere. Coming into the hallway she saw the sun, pushing through panels of stained glass by the front door. A wide coloured ray streamed from it. Caught within it dust sifted about, alive. But she was not afraid.

When she heard Hiroko moving about upstairs, she walked forward calmly. Keeping her back to the wall she crept softly up and along the passage. Hiroko was in her parents' room, the door ajar. She was tidying out a cupboard, kneeling, surrounded by shirts and underwear. Gently, Natsuko pulled the door to.

At the top of the stairs once more, she looked down into the hallway. It was strange how she no longer felt afraid, she kept thinking about it. It was as if she had stepped outside herself. She was divorced from what her hands were doing, just an observer, watching the motions of her body. Under her hand the rail was warm. Her palm was too moist to run along it and stuck to the wood. Slowly, she walked downstairs. All the time in her mind she was thinking of what there was to do, going through it again and again, so that there should be no mistake. On the last step of the stairs she stopped abruptly. For suddenly now, she no longer remembered a reason for what she was doing. There was just certain knowledge that it must be done. Nothing was more important. In the hallway the band of sunlight had stretched to swallow the long knotted fringe of a rug.

Walking purposefully, she went into the study, straight up to the fallen armour there, and looked at it anew. It was still in pieces on the floor, but arranged now in an orderly pile by Hiroko. Severed limbs were stacked in a group, the faces lay neatly, side by side. The masks stared up at Natsuko from the carpet, amputated and helpless, stripped of menace, subordinate now.

But looking at them then, remembering, calmness left her. It seemed the masks reared up, their blackness surrounding her, making one last eerie grab. She backed away then, feeling them reaching beyond her, up to the top of the house, pulling it down upon her, wrapping it tighter and tighter, until she could not breathe, until she was sure she was suffocating, her brains and bones crushed by the pressure. Into her mind flashed the spider bush in Hiroko's home, the bodies of ants marooned in gauze. She remembered the dry, hollow thorax of the moth, bound and sucked empty, pinioned for ever within the web. She knew the same death was prepared for her.

In her mind she tore and scratched at the stillness, determined it should never get her. Rushing into Hiroko's room, she dragged the heavy quilts from the cupboard into the middle of the floor: then the clothes, the blouses and underwear, and the green skirt on the hanger. Lastly she picked up the bits of shredded blouse, still lying as she had left them on the floor, and sprinkled them over the top of the pile. Her heart pumped up and down in her chest. It was still not enough. She rushed back into the kitchen, pulling out the drawer just under the sink. She knew what she wanted, but her fingers fumbled stupidly, unable to grasp the big knife. Holding it firmly she ran back into Hiroko's room. There she slashed again and again through the pile on the floor. The soft cotton innards of the quilt burst through the skin of its cover. The green skirt ripped, and great stabbed holes were left in the pages of the account book. She turned to the window and with sweeping strokes slashed the curtains also for good measure.

And then, slowly, her heart still jumping up and down wildly from her chest to her head, she went back to the study. Standing as far away as she could, bending forwards, stretching out with her arm, she pulled the knife up and down through the armour, again and again. Scratches ran over the metal, severing in places the red and blue lacings. She hacked off bits of beard and moustache and they fell, noiselessly, through the holes of the eyes, on to the carpet beneath. When she was finished she threw the knife down on top of it all and stood for a moment, breathing hard.

The creak of floorboards above her head made her start.

Then the flip-flapping of Hiroko's slippers sounded along the upstairs passage, coming towards the stairs.

In the hallway the coloured ray of light had devoured a little more of the rug. Natsuko looked back towards the study, trying to remember why she had done all she had. But in her mind was only a sureness that something ugly, old and hated was gone for ever.

There was nothing left to do. She closed the front door behind her with a soft, blunt click, and walked towards the gate.

From the corner of the road she looked up the hill and saw them, a swaying, chanting mass, coming down towards her. The men wore navy and white Summer *kimono*, the thin cotton open upon their bare chests. They staggered and rocked, chanting hypnotically to the beat of a small drum. Suddenly they were there before her, a tumult of noise, wet sweaty bodies, a tangle of muscle and leg. She saw their faces, their loose open mouths spilling out rhythmic words. Their ecstasy filled her, throbbing and boiling in her chest.

Tilting and rocking upon their shoulders was the tiered black and gold *mikoshi* shrine. It bumped majestically above them all, at its peak a brilliant gold phoenix, at its centre a secret inner shrine. Behind its shuttered gold doors was a silent black cube of emptiness, deaf to the clamour and noise.

They surrounded and passed her, drawing her into their frenzy. The chanting, bouncing mass of men, shrine, women and children closed about her, pulling her on. Her mind was blank and empty. The feelings and pictures were gone.

Once she looked over her shoulder and saw, just visible between the fir trees, the small jerking figure of Hiroko. A white smear of blouse picked her out. She was shading her eyes, looking towards the road. Suddenly she turned, running to the gate and down the steps. Natsuko knew she had been spotted. Hiroko was at the corner now, turning out on to the hill, beginning to give chase. But it all seemed distant, another landscape. And nothing to do with her.

She turned back to the Summer Festival, and followed after the crowd. Around her the colours of the hill, the sea and the sky foamed up emerald, lime, cobalt and white, stretching before her as far as she could see. And above it all hovered the phoenix, serene above the bouncing shrine, guarding the inner cube of stillness, rocking for ever beyond her reach.

KOKORO

Natsume Soseki

When the old values meet the new in Japan

In Tokyo a lonely young student from the provinces is befriended by a sophisticated older man. Yet the man himself is lonely too. For a dark shadow from his past makes him feel like a mummy left in the midst of living beings. Even the man's wife has never penetrated this tragic mystery.

Then one day the student is dramatically taken into his mentor's confidence . . .

In this beautiful, evocative portrait of Japan at the turn of the century, Natsume Soseki explores the tragic conflicts between old and new, love and duty, friendship and self-interest.

Natsume Soseki is regarded as the greatest novelist of the Meiji era, when Japan began to blend Western culture with oriental traditions.

'One of the most important Japanese writers of the modern period' *The Times Literary Supplement*

'Exquisite. The novel represents the moment at which the limitations and gifts of the native genius triumphed over an alien literature' *New York Times*

WINTER'S TALE

Mark Helprin

A haunting rhapsody of imagination –
A white horse that learns to fly
A chase that lasts one hundred years
A beautiful consumptive girl asleep on a mansion roof
A mile-long ship to build a bridge of light to infinity
An apocalyptic fire that heralds the millennium
A dazzling epic of lovers and dreamers, eccentrics and
  beauties, madmen and geniuses . . .

'Massive fantasy-saga . . . this extraordinary work,
defying synopsis, vaults time and space'
Sunday Telegraph

'Utterly extraordinary . . . a piercing sense of the
beautiful . . . funny, thoughtful, passionate'
New York Times

'Prodigiously inventive imagination and dazzling use
of words . . . a cascade of brilliant, sensuous images'
Publishers Weekly

VIRGINIE
Her Two Lives
John Hawkes

She is in her eleventh year and at the eleventh hour of her innocence. She lives in two worlds, two centuries apart; parallel lives in which dream and reality fuse as one, in which purity and decadence, innocence and knowledge, heart and mind must meet.

VIRGINIE

'Hawkes' serene, inviolable prose is so precise, luminous and evocative as to make this novel seem dreamed rather than read . . . troubling, strange, a marvel'   Angela Carter

'This is the stuff of fable and romance . . . a celebration'   *New York Times Book Review*

'Lyrical and elegant' *The Literary Review*

'A lush, erotic masterpiece' Robert Coover

'Richly ambivalent and mysterious . . .'

Washington Post

KISS OF THE SPIDER WOMAN
Manuel Puig

'Manuel Puig is one of the most consistently interesting novelists to have emerged anywhere during the past ten years.'   *The New York Times Book Review*

Prisoner 3018, Luis Alberto Molina. Sentenced July 20, 1974. Condemned to eight years' imprisonment for corruption of minors. Transferred on April 4, 1975, to Pavilion D, cell 7. Conduct good.

Detainee 16115, Valentin Arregui Paz. Arrested October 16, 1972. Held under Executive Power of the Federal Government and awaiting judgment. Transferred on April 4, 1975, to Pavilion D, cell 7. Conduct reprehensible.

Sometimes they talk all night long. In the still darkness of their cell, Molina re-weaves the glittering and fragile stories of the films he loves, and the cynical Valentin listens. Each, in his way, is a dreamer. But Valentin believes in the just cause which makes all suffering bearable; and Molina believes in the magic of romantic love which makes all else endurable. Each, in his way, has always been alonè, and always — especially now — in danger of betrayal. But in cell 7, as the long days and longer nights move inevitably on, each slowly surrenders to the other something of himself that he has never surrendered before.

'Puig dazzles one with sheer technical ability'

Newsday

'The work of a master, and a master not only of language and comedy but of feeling too'.

Sunday Times

RATES OF EXCHANGE
Malcolm Bradbury

Dr Petworth is not, it had better be admitted, a person of any great interest at all. He is white and male, forty and married, bourgeois and British — all items to anyone's contemporary discredit. He is a man to whom life has been kind, and he has paid the price for it. He teaches; that is what he does. He is also a practised cultural traveller, a man who has had diarrhoea for the British Council in almost all parts of the civilized or part-civilized world. And that is why he is here now, in the summer of 1981, in the capital city of a small dark nation known in all the history books as the bloody battlefield of central eastern Europe, travelling culturally. And preparing, though he doesn't know it — to lose more than his luggage.

'A brilliant *tour de force* . . . Superb entertainment with an underpinning of reflection and observation that makes you want instantly to read the book again'

Sunday Telegraph

'Some of the liveliest contemporary writing'

Guardian

'Rollicking, ribald, truly imaginative the way Dickens,
for example, is imaginative and real'
The Washington Post Book World

OCTOBER LIGHT
John Gardner

She has a crafty tongue, his sister, Sally Page Abbott,
even for an old woman. Might've been a preacher or a
Congressman, if the Lord in His infinite wisdom
hadn't seen fit to send her down as a female, to
minimize the risk. He'd told her that, once. After
she'd preached him a sermon off television about the
Equal Rights Amendment. 'Why, a woman ain't even
completely human,' he'd said to her. 'Look how weak
they are! Look how they cry like little children!'

It was because of foolish arguments like that that
James Page had loaded his shotgun while his sister sat
stupidly grinning into the flickering light, and without
a word of warning, he'd blown that TV screen to hell,
right back where it came from. Then he had chased
her into her room with a firewood club, and locked her
in. Let her cry. There Sally Page Abbott, eating
apples and reading an old paperback about a world of
sex, drugs and violence far from the farm, carries on
her war with her brother. But she isn't crying at all.

'Marvelous . . . John Gardner's most touching and
accessible novel'   *The New York Times*

'Dazzling . . . Profound . . . Superb . . . As rewarding
as it is entertaining'   *Los Angeles Times*